Turtle's Weir

Book Four of the Pipe Woman's Legacy

Lynne Cantwell

hearth/myth

Table of Contents

How we got here

You might not want to talk to me. I'm not making a lot of sense right now. And my part of the story isn't even the most interesting.

Still here? Well, fine. Don't say I didn't warn you.

My maiden name was Sage Curtis, but I've been Sage Orloff since Rafe and I got married fifteen years ago, in 2036. I was the darling of everyone on Earth when Rafe, Hilary Takahashi, and I figured out how to bring science and magic together in order to mitigate climate change. That fulfilled a prophecy that the Lakota Sioux goddess White Buffalo Calf Pipe Woman dropped on my great-grandfather, Looks Far Guzmán, in a vision decades ago. In that same vision, the goddess told Grandfather that my mother, Naomi Witherspoon Curtis, would pave the way for the Second Coming of all the gods by mediating a power-sharing agreement between the pagan pantheons and Jehovah. Which she did, in 2013, with the help of my father, Joseph Curtis, as her Guardian, Mom's friend Shannon McDonough as her Counselor, and an Investigator who may or may not have been a Chicano guy named Juan Riberas, a.k.a. Jack Rivers. Rivers was a difficult son of a bitch, by all accounts, and he seemed to have disappeared off the face of the Earth right after the gods came back.

If you think that's complicated, stick around. It gets worse.

There appears to have been a further bit of prophecy, which the goddess didn't bother telling anybody about until she divulged the information to my mother a couple of years ago. It seems Earth's Savior – that's me, for better or worse – is supposed to produce an Heir. And the Heir is supposed to reign as the gods' representative on Earth after They leave again. Which apparently is going to be soonish.

When Mom told me, we had a little falling out over it. Okay, fine – we had a big ol' fucking fight. Rafe and I work for a government organization based in Washington, D.C., called the United States

Joint Defense Force, Hominid/Deific – which sounds like it's part of the military but it's not, really. Well, it kind of is. It's complicated. And it's mostly top secret. You wouldn't believe the hoops Rafe and I had to jump through to get clearance.

Anyway, the two of us are not in a good place right now to have a baby, for several reasons, and I told my mother this. But Mom isn't good with hearing the word *no*. So there was a period of time while I wasn't speaking to her. It's only been recently that we've been reconciled – say, within the past few weeks – and that happened only because my therapist told me to. Well, and also, Mom has cancer, and it's terminal. Although my brother Webb isn't buying the diagnosis. But being Webb, he won't tell anybody why.

Oh, right – Webb. See, I'm allied with the Lakota spirit Thunderbird, and Webb has always been my *heyoka* – my Sacred Clown. He knows the future (unless he's directly involved) and he's practically forced to speak truth to power, especially if it involves making everything into a big fucking joke.

Sorry. Even though we're grown now – he's thirty-five and I'm thirty-eight – he can still annoy me.

He did manage to break out of the annoying-little-brother mold earlier this fall, though. A group called the National Neo-Atheists Movement had put out a series of videos that painted my mother in a less-than-flattering light. All right, they made her look like a hooker, which isn't true at all. But anyway, they had set up their video production facility in the New Mexican desert, and they'd also set up a throwback commune in the mountains of Georgia. Rafe and I were sent to infiltrate the commune. It was all very 1950s, with the men In Charge and the women basically their chattel. Things got pretty bad there – I was raped and Rafe was forced to have sex with one of the wives – and I ended up setting fire to the place with my eyes to get us out. We're both still wrapping our heads around what happened there. Which is a big reason why having a baby right now would be a Bad Idea.

But it was Webb who took out the video production facility – and when he kicked over that rock, Jack Rivers slithered out. Rivers, I hear, is not entirely sane, which made it easy for this demigod, Lucifer, to make him a tool. Our family had gone up against Lucifer once before, when Webb and I were just kids. Anyway, this time Webb made a cage of sorts for Lucifer – which was a good trick considering Lucifer was made of smoke – and then destroyed the cage. Webb says we won't be bothered by him again.

Lucifer's handler, though, was the Norse Trickster Loki, and He has managed to start the countdown clock to Ragnarok – the gods' doom. We're not sure whether that means Earth will be destroyed, or only the part of the gods' world where the Norse pantheon holds sway. Regardless, we have heard that it's pretty chaotic in the gods' world right now, and They're expecting Mom to go there and mediate a new power-sharing agreement – even though she's sick, and even though White Buffalo Calf Pipe Woman seems to have abandoned her.

Mom wants Webb to help her with the mediation – but my old college roommate Hilary is pregnant with his baby, and he's waiting to hear back about a grant, so his plate is pretty full right now. On the other hand, Mom can be pretty persuasive. On the *other* other hand, Webb can be pretty stubborn. Mom says he gets it from Dad.

Before Mom can conduct the mediation, we have to find a way into the gods' realm. Loki has the portals locked down tight, but Webb thinks he knows a way in, and Rafe has been all hot to go out to the desert and help. I told him to go ahead, thinking it would give me time alone to get better. But then our boss, Darrell Warren, sent him out on a new project.

Maybe Webb hasn't pestered me for the last few weeks because he knew Rafe would be too busy to go now. I dunno.

I almost forgot to mention two things. The first one is that we don't know where Jack Rivers is. The second one is that there's a hereditary Icelandic princess named Ingrid Ingunnardottir whose state visit to Colorado keeps getting extended. She seems to have taken a shine to Rex Holt, the eldest son of former President Brock Holt (to whom my mother was briefly engaged, once upon a time) and his wife, Antonia Greco. Mom and Dad like Ingrid a lot, and Mom says she and Rex would make beautiful babies.

Even though we're talking again, I wish she'd shut up about the baby stuff.

But anyway, it's up to Webb now. My therapist says I'm getting better, but I know in my heart that I'm not in any shape to help.

But I wonder why I haven't heard from him?

Chapter 1

I'm sure you've heard the phrase, "Out of sight, out of mind." Well, when Tricksters are involved, it's even more likely that whatever's out of sight will slip one's mind – even when the mind in question is inside another Trickster's head.

Which is how I managed to forget about my vow to find a way into the gods' realm and track down the goddess responsible for my mother's illness.

It's partially my fault. As Sage mentioned, I was waiting to hear back from the committee charged with the fate of my grant application to fund development and construction of a fairytale castle in the Rockies – an art installation that would eventually degrade and dissolve until it was nothing but a memory. Waiting has never been a strength of mine. It's kind of a family failing, actually. But in any case, I forced myself to forget about the grant, and the project, and the fact that I had at least six weeks, until November 30th, before I could expect to hear anything – and that was only if they rejected my project out of hand. Debate over the finalists would take an additional couple of weeks. The winner was to be announced December 15th.

Foolishly, perhaps, I had staked my professional future on this one grant. If I won, it would make me the family breadwinner for the first time since my girlfriend Hilary and I had moved in together – which was kind of important, since our baby was due just before Christmas. It was bad enough that I was still paying rent to my parents at the age of thirty-five.

My point is that I didn't want to dwell on the grant process, so I forced myself to think of other things. But that little mind trick opened a crack in my psychic defenses, and I found myself forgetting other important stuff, too. Like how sick my mother's cancer was making her. And how angry Loki had been when I informed Him that I'd dispatched Lucifer from the Earth for good. And why the gods hadn't been around in a while.

However, as Sage also mentioned, Ingrid was still around. Her state visit was only supposed to last a week; it had included a reception at the Denver home of our former President, Brock Holt, and his family, which Mom and I had attended. But her visit was now going on four weeks in the U.S., three of them in Colorado. The official story was that she was negotiating some kind of reciprocal tourism thing. But it was clear to everyone in my family, at least, that her real goal was to get cozy with the President's number-one son. Sage and I had pretty much known Rex and his younger brother, Roman, all our lives. I thought Rex was an airhead wrapped in a mantle of political ambition, but Ingrid seemed to adore him, and the feeling was apparently mutual. I did wonder whether Rex ever dropped his newly-acquired baritone speaking voice when they were alone together, but I didn't care enough to research it.

As for Roman, Mom said he would have been a hippie if he'd grown up in the 1960s. He wore raggedy sweaters, played boogie-woogie piano, and generally behaved as if he didn't give a damn what anyone thought of him. Every now and then, though, I'd remember something about him that had something to do with an offer to help me with…something. I couldn't quite put my finger on what it was he had said, or what he expected me to do. My mind simply skittered away from the subject, and I'd find myself thinking about Ingrid and Rex making mooncalf eyes at each other.

Then sometimes, another memory would nag at me – a fanciful one in which Ingrid unhinged her jaws as if she intended to swallow me whole – but it would be there and gone in an instant, and I'd shake my head at my moment of terror and wonder what Hilary and I were having for supper, or something.

While I was experiencing these occasional descents into unreality, life went on. Hilary began to walk with one hand on the small of her back, as if her arm were a counterweight to her swelling belly. Aunt Shannon, Mom's best friend, began stopping by every few days, until Hilary laughed in resignation and agreed to let her be our midwife.

Aunt Shannon also brought us the latest news about Mom, which we weren't always guaranteed to get from my parents. Her condition was still grave, but hadn't worsened. Still, Aunt Shannon would shake her head. "I just can't figure it out," she said to us one night, about a week before Thanksgiving. "I've been talking online with some holistic healers and..."

"Holistic?" I said. "For cancer?"

"Yes, holistic," she said. "And yes, for cancer. There's almost always an emotional or spiritual component to disease, and it can affect the efficacy of treatment." She was a therapist as well as a midwife.

I flashed briefly on a memory of my mother looking pale and drawn during – a virtual meeting? And was Sage and Rafe's boss, Darrell Warren, there? Anyway, the mental picture disappeared while Aunt Shannon was still talking.

"I've been trying a new therapy, based on something one of them said. It should work. And it does, briefly – there's measurable improvement. Her tumors start to shrink. The oncologist confirms it. And then we're right back where we started from." Her eyes glistened with frustration.

Another vague memory prompted me to say, "That's happened before, hasn't it?"

She eyed me. "It's been happening for at least a year." She closed her eyes and clenched her hands into fists. "It's like someone is reaching in and undoing everything I do."

I opened my mouth, but the words fled before I could give voice to them. Instead, I heard myself say, "Would you like to stay for supper?"

This went on for several weeks – almost until Thanksgiving.

We always celebrated at Mom and Dad's house in Golden, Colorado, in the foothills of the Rockies. Sage and Rafe always flew in from Washington, and planned to do so again this year, although Sage was coming on an earlier flight. She had been on medical leave for about a month while she wrestled with emotional demons, figuratively speaking, that were awakened during the debacle in Georgia, but she had recently been cleared to go back to work part-time. Rafe was out in the field on a new assignment, and would be along on Thanksgiving Eve. "You'll pay through the nose for that ticket," I said when he outlined their plans to me on Skype. "Assuming you can get a seat at all."

"It'll work out," he said. "If I can't get a flight, I'll fly." He wasn't joking; Rafe, Sage, and my father are all shapeshifters. Dad can be pretty much any animal, but Sage and Rafe's talents are more limited: Rafe morphs into a raven, and my sister becomes a Thunderbird.

I was glad they were coming at all, and that Mom and Sage were at least talking again.

Even Grandma Witherspoon was coming. Now in her nineties and having outlived Grandpa Drew, she and my great-aunt Hannah were keeping house together on the Pine Ridge Reservation in South Dakota. My parents had managed to keep the news of Mom's illness from Grandma, but as soon as she found out, she talked my cousin Leonard into driving her to Denver. They were to arrive the weekend before the big day, so Grandma could help Mom and Sage cook. Hilary thought it over for about half a second, and offered to referee.

At first, I was kind of excited to have the house in Boulder to myself; after all, it might have been the last bit of peace I got before the baby came. But then I thought about how I would likely be rattling around the place, ghosting from room to room, and eating a lot of takeout, and decided to go with Hilary. I figured at least there would be entertainment in Golden if Sage's laser eyes lit up.

With Mom sick and Dad unwilling to drive with passengers in the car, I was pressed into service as chauffeur. Sage arrived Sunday afternoon. She came to the curb at DIA pushing two massive suitcases on a cart. "I brought some of Rafe's stuff, in case he has to travel light on Wednesday," she explained as I hefted them into the back of Dad's hovercar.

"Which of the suitcases is his?"

She tossed in the backpack she'd been wearing and gave me an embarrassed smile. "Actually, neither one. His stuff is in the backpack." Then she crossed her arms and eyed me critically.

I eyed her right back. "What?"

"You don't look any different."

"Am I supposed to?"

She shrugged. "I thought maybe you'd be wearing a new-father glow, or something."

I slammed the trunk. "I'm not a father yet. Maybe that explains it."

"Is Hilary glowing?"

"No, Sage," I said with exaggerated patience. "That's Mom's thing. Remember?" Our mother has, on occasion, glowed with an argent fire of righteousness – although it hadn't happened in years.

She gave me a quick hug and got in the car. "You look good," she offered as we made our way onto Peña Boulevard. She gazed at the suburban tract housing on either side of the road. "Gods. Remember when this was nothing but prairie? You could see all the way to Grandfather's wickiup, almost."

"I remember," I said. "And you look good, too." Her usual severe expression was gone; the muscles of her face were more relaxed, although I could still detect the *v* between her eyebrows from her habitual frown. Her face looked thinner than I remembered, which was understandable, given what she'd been through over the past few months. But her posture still reminded me of a coiled spring: stored energy, ready to leap into action at the slightest provocation.

She nodded once at my compliment, still taking in our surroundings. But when I punched up the hover function, I got her attention immediately. "Toll's going to be kind of pricey today, won't it? With all this traffic?" She nodded at the line of brake lights in front of us – well, below us, now.

I tapped the little box stuck to the windshield. "Dad's paying the freight, not me. And I'm sure he'd like to see you before Thanksgiving's over."

In response, she looked out the window again. "I hope I don't disappoint them," she said softly.

"Cut it out," I said. "The only person who's ever been disappointed in you is you."

She snorted and cut a glance at me. "And Rafe. And Darrell."

"Bullshit," I said. But she acted as if she hadn't heard me. I shook my head and concentrated on driving.

Dad met us at the front door. Sage walked into his arms and stayed there while I brought in her suitcases and stuff. Then I spied Mom in the doorway to the kitchen, and went over to her. "Come here," I said, letting her lean on me. "Let me introduce you to my sister."

Mom laughed – which is what I was after, of course – and smacked my shoulder. Then she let me take her to Dad and Sage, whereupon I called out, "Group hug!" like a six-year-old and shoved us in between them.

Despite my antics, nobody got out of there with dry eyes. I had to admit, it was good to feel like a family again. Even though I was pretty sure it wouldn't last.

Eventually, I broke the huddle. "I'll help you take the stuff to your room," I told Sage, as I grabbed the backpack and headed for the stairs.

"Hey! What about the suitcases?"

I was already halfway up. "You said that was all *your* stuff. You know Mom's rule – if you can't carry it, don't bring it."

Sage turned to Mom for backup, but I was already on my way down. "Kidding," I said as I passed my sister and hefted one of her bags.

"You bet your ass you're kidding," she shot back as she took the other one and came after me.

"Don't fry anything, you two," Dad said, laughter in his voice, as we ran up the stairs.

We met Hilary in the hall on our way back down, and another round of hugs ensued. "You lied to me, little brother," Sage said as she admired my girlfriend's roundness. "She is too glowing."

"Maybe," I said. "But not the way Mom does it." I grinned at Sage and pulled Hilary against me.

"Thank the gods for that," said Hilary. She has never lost her Carolina accent, which is great, because I love it. "I'm tangled up in your family business enough as it is." She took one of Sage's hands. "I'm so glad you're here."

"So am I," she said. But it sounded a little like she was still convincing herself it was true.

Leonard and Grandma arrived just before suppertime. Grandma immediately went into medical mode, latching onto Mom and Hilary and peppering them with questions about symptoms and treatments. Dad sat in his usual chair, looking bemused, while Hilary and Sage took over the task of getting the food ready. I offered to help, but Hilary waved me off. "We got this," she said, making shooing motions with one hand.

That left me with my cousin. Leonard Sauvage was broad-shouldered and brown-skinned, but his hair had gone salt-and-pepper since I'd seen him last. He still wore it in a long braid down his back, though. Leonard was a Wolf Dreamer — a respected elder in his *tiyošpaye*, or district, of the Lakota tribe. He'd taught me a lot about survival, and about the best ways to use my *heyoka* skills so that my life would stay in balance.

Now, he looked hard at me. "I'm surprised I haven't heard from you."

I blinked. "Was I supposed to call you or something?"

His eyes widened. "You did mean to take me along when you went looking for the entrance to the gods' realm, didn't you? I didn't dream that conversation, did I?"

"Oh," I said faintly. "Yeah." Now that he mentioned it, I did recall contacting him right after the most recent crisis, and we did talk about going somewhere. To find a thing. Or a place. And it had something to do with the gods.

"Weren't you in kind of a rush?"

I stared off into space. "I don't think so…"

"Webb," he said, and laid a hand on my shoulder. "What's gotten into you? You were ready to go the last time we spoke. I figured I'd get a call within a day or two, so I put some things on hold. But that was more than a month ago."

I shook my head. I was having trouble remembering the gist of our conversation.

He frowned. Then he seemed to go inside himself for a moment. When his eyes focused again, he looked over my shoulder and said, "Hey, Joseph. You think that's going to be enough firewood?"

Dad looked at the woodpile next to the fireplace and shrugged. "We could use a few more logs, I guess."

Leonard nodded toward the back door. "We'll go get some. Come on, Webb."

The sun had dropped below the mountaintops, and the air tasted of snow. I led Leonard to the woodpile at the end of the deck. As we bent to pick up the logs, I saw something move in the shadows on the other side of the pile, and stiffened. Leonard, instantly alert, looked in the direction I pointed.

A specter was rising from behind the stack of logs. No, it wasn't a specter – it was an Indian wrapped in an old-fashioned chief's blanket.

"Iktomi," Leonard said quietly in greeting.

The Lakota Trickster rarely took human form, preferring instead to appear as a spider. In fact, I could remember only one other time when I'd seen Him as I did now.

He ignored my cousin, focusing instead on me. "Webb!" he rasped. "Why haven't you come?"

"Come where?" I asked.

Iktomi searched me, eyes narrowed. "There's a glamor on him," He said, addressing Leonard. "See it?"

Leonard squinted at a spot just above my head. "Yes," he said with a nod. "That explains a lot."

"You know what to do?" Iktomi asked.

"I'm standing right here, y'know," I said.

But Leonard went on ignoring me as he nodded to the god.

Iktomi grunted and turned to me at last. "You must *focus*, Webb. Ragnarok is nearly here. Already, it's god against god. We need your mother's help to avert a disaster. *Focus!*"

At that, Leonard used one of the logs he was holding to hit me in the forehead.

I dropped like a sack of potatoes. But I didn't pass out – the whack wasn't hard enough for that. Instead, I blinked several times, and suddenly I remembered everything: my dreams of Ingrid, Mom falling during the reception at the Holts', my conversation with Spider Grandmother – everything. Even my little golden spider pal, who – come to think of it – I hadn't seen since we caged Lucifer and put him away permanently.

I also remembered, with mounting chagrin, how Mom and Dad had been unable to focus on anything I said about Ingrid and how she might be behind my mother's illness. That should have put me on alert, but it didn't. And somehow, she'd extended her glamor over them to me, too.

As Leonard helped me up, I noticed two things: Iktomi was gone; and at the end of the woodpile closest to the house, stretched between the logs and the deck railing, was an enormous spider web, its strands glimmering in the porch light. Woven into the web was the word FOCUS in big, block letters.

"Oh, my gods," I said. "We've got work to do. And fast. We've already lost too much time."

Chapter 2

I hoped we wouldn't need the log-to-forehead trick to pull my parents out from under Ingrid's influence, but it didn't look promising. Leonard and I sat everybody down in the family room and tried to talk to Mom and Dad about it, but they looked at us as if we were speaking another language.

Then Sage said, "This sounds like the thing Rafe has been working on for Darrell."

"It does?" I said. "You got any more info?"

She shook her head. "It's classified. I don't even think I'm supposed to know. But he mentioned that there's some kind of magical blackout affecting certain parts of the world, and it may be connected to the group of individuals he and I were investigating last month."

"The Neo-Atheists?" Dad said. "I thought you had broken them up."

"So did I." She shook her head and lapsed into a grim silence.

Dad hugged Sage and looked at Mom. "Jack," he said. "I'd bet money that bastard is involved."

"You're always blaming him," she snapped. "He's old and sick. Why can't you leave him alone?"

"Why can't he leave *us* alone?" Dad said. "That was the deal, Naomi. Remember?"

She glared at him. "He *has* left us alone until now. That's why I don't want to rush to judgment against him. There must be someone behind him. Pushing him."

"I'd bet it's the same power that's pushing Ingrid," I said, and again got the deer-in-the-headlights look from both of my parents. I sighed and turned to Leonard. "We need to figure out how Ingrid is doing this, so we can turn it off."

"Or figure out some protection against it," he said.

"Helmets," Sage said.

I blinked at her.

"You remember," she said. "The dream helmet you made me when I was worried about flying in my sleep."

Sage had come into her powers of flight abruptly, when she was thirteen and I was ten. She'd had a few dreams in which she thought she was flying – and then, one night, she actually sleepwalked out the back door, took wing, and freaked out when she woke up in a tree. I made her a helmet out of bright orange yarn. I never knew precisely how the thing worked – whether it really did keep her dreams inside her head, as I told her it would, or whether she simply believed that it did – but she never sleep-flew again. "Oh, right," I said now. "Yeah, that would work. But I think an amulet would be more discreet. And I still need to know what I'm protecting us against." I looked at Leonard. "Want to take a trip with me?"

"After supper," said Hilary, turning from the stove. "It's ready. Everybody come and grab a bowl."

As the others lined up obediently for chili and cornbread, I hugged my girlfriend from behind. "Baby, you're the greatest," I said in her ear, my voice pitched low, and nuzzled her neck.

She giggled and squirmed away. "Go get some dinner, lover boy."

I stole a kiss and got back in line behind Grandma, who was watching the two of us like a bird of prey. "When are you kids going to make it legal?" she asked me. Her tone was light, but there was a rod of steel underneath the joshing.

"Um," I said, exchanging a guilty look with Hilary. "We haven't actually talked about it."

"But you and I have talked about it," my mother, the lawyer, chimed in. "And I've told you it would be a good idea. Marriage grants specific legal rights that can be helpful to couples, especially when children are involved."

Grandma snorted and looked pointedly at Mom. "Listen to you. If I hadn't shown up when I did, you and Joseph might not be married yet."

Mom turned a faint pink. "We would have gotten around to it eventually," she said.

"We *were* kind of busy at the time," Dad said around a mouthful of cornbread. "Getting the gods to agree to share power, and all."

Grandma turned her gaze back to me. "So history is repeating itself. Is that it?"

"Something like that," I mumbled.

"Webb's waiting to hear back about his grant, Grandma," Hilary said. "He wants to have a steady source of income for us. That's a good thing, isn't it? You want that for your great-grandchild, don't you?"

A delighted smile spread slowly across my face. My sweet, shy girlfriend, who could be self-effacing to a fault, was actually standing up to my grandmother.

But Grandma wasn't about to back down. She reached the head of the line and planted her hands on her hips. "Of course I do. But what happens if he doesn't get the grant?"

Hilary planted her free hand on her own hip – the other was still holding the ladle over the chili pot – and said, "He will."

"Hotaru," I said gently, calling Hilary by her Japanese name. Her faith in me was gratifying, but we both knew I might not win.

"You *will*," she said, as if it were a prophecy. "And then we'll get married. All y'all will be invited." She gestured to the room. "And Grandma, Webb will dance the first dance with you."

What could I do? She was on a roll. "Second dance," I said. "The first spot on my dance card is already taken." I grinned at Hilary, who relaxed enough to smile back at me. "Sorry, Grandma."

She shot us both a look that said *we'll see about that* and snatched the ladle out of Hilary's hand to fill her own bowl. As she seated herself, she said, "I'm taking you two at your word, you know."

"You do that," I said, and gave the cook another smooch.

"About that trip," Leonard said as he and I cleaned up from supper. Dad had gone for a run. I could hear the rest of the family chatting in the living room, whence we'd banished them while my cousin and I tidied up. I expected the older folks to begin nodding off shortly, and maybe Sage, too, as her body clock was still on East Coast time.

"What about it?" I responded as I washed out the chili pot.

"Where are we going?"

I tapped my temple with a soapy finger. "You remember how to do it?"

He laughed outright. He was the one who had taught me.

A few minutes later, when everything was clean and put away, we adjourned to the family room fireplace. I brought along a couple of mugs of coffee; Leonard said he wouldn't need it, but I always found caffeine useful as a pick-me-up afterward.

We situated ourselves, cross-legged, before the crackling flames. Leonard began a heartbeat chant, and I joined him in it. I usually didn't bother with the chant – I was adept enough to slide into the timestream without it – but I wanted us united so that we ended up at the same place.

The flames danced inside my closed eyelids, leaping in time to the beat of our chant. Then I slid through the wall of flame as if it were nothing but a light show – and there before me, above and below and all around, was the splendor of the Universal web.

I took a moment, as always, to appreciate the artistry that had gone into it. I was good at making simulations of the web, but nowhere near as good as whoever had woven this. Layers of strands glimmered gold, green, silver, indigo, and every other color you can think of – as well as many no one's ever thought of. In places, a couple or a few or many stands intertwined – some for a short distance, others for what might constitute a lifetime. Sometimes a strand quivered away from another; if you looked carefully, you could see where those two strands had either joined before or would join farther along, and oftentimes that joining was fraught with tangles. Other strands reached for many, or for none, and yet even the solitary strands often had a foundation of support from others.

If you could get high enough above the web – which I did, once – you could trace the fate of whole civilizations. And you could see how some strands looped back onto themselves, or transformed into a whole new strand. There was room for both death and rebirth in this colossal web, because nothing ever actually ended. Time here was a circle. Everything was connected to everything else, and what happened before would indeed happen again.

And yet, this too was a simulation. No one could see the real web, except maybe the gods, and maybe not even Them. For a particularly glittering portion of this web looked very much like the gods' realm. I wondered whether we could use the web to get into their realm – and then set the idea aside to ponder later, for my old friend, the glowing golden spider, was bouncing about in a tiny doorway well above my head.

I should have had trouble reaching the doorway, but thankfully, the laws of physics didn't apply here. I crouched and sprang, and landed neatly beside him. He leapt to my shoulder and I high-fived him gently. "Good to see you, buddy," I said. "I brought a friend along. Do you see him?"

As I spoke, I looked out at the web. There was Leonard, walking up an incline toward us. I beckoned him in and shut the door.

We were in my own, much smaller, simulation of the Universal web. Again, I'd gone for the timestream design, since I was comfortable with it; now I was glad I had, because it was the first design Leonard had taught me. He looked around, nodding in satisfaction. "I like what you've done with the place," he said.

"Practice makes perfect," I said with a proud grin. "Let's see if we can find out what's going on."

My cousin was already scanning the timestreams I'd captured. "I'm not seeing anything obvious. Maybe if we isolate the family's streams…?"

"I don't think that will help. The effects seem to be geographic rather than family-related," I said. "You remembered my phone call just fine. And Sage isn't having any trouble remembering what she went through."

"For good or ill," he said. "She seems distant. Is she okay?"

As much as I wanted to help my sister, it wasn't why we were here. "She's getting help," I said, and squinted at Mom's timestream. "What am I looking for here? What does a glamor look like?"

He shrugged. "Depends on the type. Sometimes they add a little shimmer, a little glow. Sometimes they're not much more than a shadow."

"You're a lot of help," I said. "Does the appearance differ if the glamor is cast over more than one stream?"

"That's a good question. I'm not sure I've ever seen one like that. Most of the time they're directed at a single individual." I was about to complain again, when he pointed to the stream adjoining my mother's. "Isn't that Uncle Joseph's stream?"

"Yeah, it is."

"What *is* that?"

I saw what he meant, kind of. There was something there. Squinting wasn't helping, so instead I relaxed and looked with an inner sight – and it popped into bold relief. "What the heck…?" I said. "*Enkou?*"

Sure enough, my girlfriend's kappa, or Japanese water demon, was busily constructing something along one side of my father's timestream. I dove toward him, my spider buddy hanging onto my sleeve. When we were within shouting range, I slowed our descent and called, "What are you doing in here?"

"Hello, Webb. Build weir," he said, busily shoring up what looked for all the world like a mud embankment.

"What's it for?"

He nodded upstream, careful not to let any of the water in his head concavity slosh out. "Dark," was all he said, before going back to work.

Sure enough, dots of darkness stretched across my father's timestream. I realized now why I hadn't seen them from above: they were too small, and spaced too far apart, to be visible from so far away. I glanced at my mother's timestream, and saw the same cloud of tiny dots of darkness marching back along it. In places, it looked as if the grid of dots had been mended.

As Leonard landed beside me, I reached out and caught one of the dots from the side of my father's timestream. It shuddered in my hand, then fought hard against my grip. A moment more, and it went quiescent…and melted.

"Ice," I said, letting the water trickle onto the dirt at my feet. Enkou had crossed to the other side of the stream and had begun to build up the embankment there. "You're going to build an ice dam," I said. "Why?"

"Joseph needs clear head," he said, stomping on his wall of mud to firm it up.

"What about my mother?" I said. "She needs to have a clear head, too! She's the one who needs to negotiate the new power-sharing agreement."

"Naomi has other problem. First Joseph. Easy fix. Then work on Naomi."

He was right, of course. The amnesia was separate from my mother's illness. "Hang on," I said to Leonard. "I want to take a better look at something." I sprang aloft and traveled back along my parents' timestreams for some distance. I had wanted to take a close look at my mother's weeks before, but Lucifer had shown up and blocked my access. That wasn't going to be a problem today.

Sure enough, the ice dots were a relatively recent phenomenon; if I dove into the timestream at their start, I was certain I would be at the reception where Mom and I met Ingrid. There were only a couple of mended places; I surmised those were from Aunt Shannon's most recent attempts to cure Mom's cancer.

The dots above my father's timestream started a hair's breadth later than the ones above my mother's; I dove into his stream, and found myself riding in Dad's SUV with me at the wheel and Dad riding shotgun, at the precise moment when I'd first mentioned Ingrid to him.

Cursing silently, I surfaced and dove into Mom's timestream where the dots began. I'd been wrong. They didn't start while we were at the reception; they started afterward, when I was driving her home. When I took her hand and asked her what had caused her to fall.

I jumped back to my conversation in the car with Dad. Had I touched him? Yeah, I had. My hand on the gearshift lever had grazed his knee.

I was Typhoid Mary. Ingrid had dropped the spell on me at the party, and I'd infected my parents.

I surfaced urgently and glanced around for my own timestream. There it was, and there were the tiny dots hovering above. I dove in at their start – and found myself at the reception at the Holts'. Ingrid was letting go of my hand and reaching for my mother's as President Holt introduced them. I felt again the sickening jolt as time slowed to a crawl. Webb-in-the-timeline reached out to bat Mom's hand away – and from this vantage point, I could see the tiny, dark spots concentrated on my palm where Ingrid had touched me, and the spot of darkness that flowed from her to Mom when they shook hands. That spot flowed down Mom's leg as she stepped away, and tangled around her ankles.

I'd been right. Ingrid was responsible for Mom's fall.

As Webb-in-the-timeline broke from the bar to scramble toward Mom, I glanced around the room. Ingrid watched what she had wrought with satisfaction in her eye. But then she glanced up from the tableau on the rug at me – not Webb-in-the-timeline, but *me*, Webb-the-observer. Her eyebrows shot up and her mouth dropped open. Then her forehead creased in anger.

I covered my own shock with a jaunty little wave. Then, as I got ready to spring up out of the timestream, I realized someone else in the room was watching me: Roman Holt. He was crouched next to me on the floor, holding my drink and Mom's. And of the three of us

– Roman, Ingrid, and me – he was the only one who didn't look surprised that I was there.

In real life, right after he'd handed us our drinks, he'd told me, *I'm here to help. Remember that.* The comment had seemed to come from out of the blue at the time. Now, at least, I had a little context.

I gave him a shrug and a grin, and got out of there.

Seconds later, I landed next to Leonard. Enkou was still busy building his weir. "This is all my fault," I said, panting as if I'd run a marathon. "We need to bring Sage in here. She can melt the ice with her eyes."

"And do what other damage?" Leonard said reasonably.

"You don't get it," I said. "I'm the one who started all this. Ingrid infected me, and I gave it to Mom and Dad."

"Then it's Ingrid who we have to stop," he said.

I glanced at my timeline. "We need to do it soon," I said, nodding to where new tiny dots were forming to fill in a hole above it. "I'm already starting to forget everything again."

"Webb, listen to me," Leonard said, putting a heavy hand on my shoulder. "You're starting to panic. That isn't going to help."

I swallowed hard. "Okay. Okay."

When he saw that I was calmer, he said, "We came here with two purposes, right? Tell me what they were."

"To find out how Ingrid is controlling our memories, and to figure out a way to stop her."

"Good. Now. You figured out how she's doing it, so we're halfway there."

"Right."

"And we know we can't stop her from doing it, because it's already been done."

I saw what he meant by that. We were all infected weeks ago. "What we need is a cure," I said.

"Right."

"Which is why we need Sage," I said.

Leonard gripped my shoulder hard. "*Think*, Webb. You can't have rogue laser beams ricocheting around in here. Think of the damage they could do."

"This is just a simulation," I argued.

"Then burning away the ice here won't help us in the real world anyway," he said. "And you *really* don't want to let a Thunderbird loose on the web out there."

He was right; that would be a spectacularly bad idea. My shoulders sagged. "Then what?" I asked. "I'm out of solutions."

"No, you're not. You were on the right track a minute ago. What we're fighting isn't ice – not at its root."

I remembered the shadowed thing slithering down my mother's leg. "What we're fighting is darkness," I said.

"You need light for that," said a voice I recognized. I spun, nearly slipping down the muddy bank, to confront him. "Hey, Webb," Roman Holt said. "I thought I'd find you here."

"How did you get in?" I demanded. I was starting to lose my cool again. How were all these people finding their way into my head? First Loki, then Lucifer, and now Roman. Was my head that porous?

Did that mean Ingrid could find her way in here, too?

"Everybody out!" I said. "I need to shut this thing down."

"Easy there," Roman said, with a hand on my shoulder. "No need to go to extremes. I didn't penetrate your force field. Your little buddy let me in." He nodded to his own shoulder, where the glowing spider clung to his tattered Aran sweater. He scampered down Roman's arm and jumped to mine.

"Traitor," I said as he spun a line and swung himself up into my hair. "Don't think I can't find you up there."

"It's cool, really. I'm a friend." His self-deprecating grin in place, he stuck out a hand in Leonard's direction. "Hey there, nice to meet you. I'm Roman Holt."

Leonard shook his hand silently, his expression unreadable.

"Tell me something, Roman," I said. "You saw me at the reception for Ingrid."

He swooped his bangs out of his eyes with one hand and laughed. "Well, yeah," he said. "You were there with your mom."

"No, that's not what I mean. I mean you saw me after Mom fell. You were next to Mom and me on the floor, and you looked up and saw me watching it all."

He raised his eyebrows.

"How did you do that?"

"How did you know?" He seemed genuinely baffled.

"I saw it in the timestream just now."

"Dude," he said, drawing out the *u* like an '80s stoner. "You can do that? Wow."

"Roman," I said evenly. "How. Did. You. Do. It?"

"I dunno," he said. "I saw Ingrid looking at something, so I looked where she was looking and saw it was you."

"But how…?" I closed my eyes for a moment, and changed tactics. "Look. You say you're a friend. I want to believe you. The gods know I could use a friend. But the only other…entity…who has made it into this simulation without an express invitation from me has been Loki." And Lucifer, but we didn't need to get into that. "Now, that time in your parents' TV studio when Tess Showalter was interviewing our mothers, you told me to go behind a curtain, and who did I bump into there but Loki? And oddly enough, the last time I ran into Loki was at the reception for Ingrid, which is also the last time I saw *you*.

"How do I know Loki didn't send you here today? How do I know He didn't let you in? How do I know you're not in league with Ingrid?"

"That bitch," he hissed through clenched teeth.

With that, I relaxed. But not a lot. "All right, that's a start," I said. "But you still need to give me a reason to trust you."

Roman dropped his head for a moment. When he brought it back up, his whole demeanor had changed. Gone was the carefree boogie-woogie piano player; in his place was a deadly serious man with steel-gray eyes. "Hermes," he said.

"What about Hermes?" Leonard asked, his own eyes narrowed.

But my brain was already tearing through the associations and what they might mean. "You're allied with Hermes," I said. "The messenger of the gods." At his nod, I said, "Do you have a message from Them for us?"

"It doesn't work that way," he said impatiently. "Would you please tell the kappa to stop that? It's distracting, and anyway it won't help."

"Enkou!" I called, but Hilary's ninja turtle refused to acknowledge me. I shrugged. "Sorry. He's Hilary's, not mine. You were saying?"

He cast such a murderous glance at Enkou that I began to think I liked the old Roman better. Then he turned to me. "I am not 'in league with Loki,' as you put it. On the day of the interview, I happened to see Him and my father skulking around on the grounds outside, waiting for your mother to show up, so they could make their big entrance. None of us had any idea *you* were coming. Nor did I know Loki was behind the curtain. I really did send you back there to confirm that there was no exterior door. Loki must have translated them both into the studio."

Plausible, as far as it went. "I still want to know what you're doing in here."

"Loki didn't send me, if that's what you're asking," he said, his voice harsh. "I don't have any use for that old Trickster."

"He got your father elected President," I said.

"Yes, and He got him in trouble, too," Roman said. "He stirred the pot overseas to get us into war more than once, because it pleased Him to cause trouble. And He's the one who let Lucifer out."

"I know that," I said. "You still haven't answered my question. What are you doing in here?"

"I have a message for you," he said.

"That may be why," I said, "but not how. Come on, Roman, or this goes no further."

At last, he said, "I told you. Your little buddy let me in before you even got here." He pointed at my hair. "He was my little buddy first."

I remembered then where I'd first seen the glowing spider: in the dining room of the Holts' residence. "Oh, gods," I said, chagrined. "I had no idea. I swear I didn't take him deliberately – he just tagged along with me."

Roman shrugged, something of his normal demeanor back in place. "It's okay. He's a free agent." Then the steely-eyed look was back. "Do you want to hear the message?"

I shrugged. "Sure."

"Ingrid's goddess has it in for your mother," he said. "But you're going to have to go into the gods' realm to confront Her."

"We'd figured that much out," I said. "What we don't know is which goddess is making my mother sick. Is it Freya?"

He snorted. "Freya! Who told you that? Loki?"

"Yeah, and I didn't believe Him."

"Good for you," Roman said. "It's not Freya. But She knows who it is."

"And She's in the gods' realm." I sighed. "Which puts us right back where we started. I have a notion of where an entrance might be, down in the southwestern corner of Colorado."

"The *sipapu*," he said instantly. "Good guess. Yes. That's one Hermes sometimes used, especially after the one near Boulder was blocked off."

My excitement rose. "Do you know which *sipapu* is the one we're looking for?"

"No. But I know someone who does."

"We would very much like to meet him or her." I looked at Leonard, who nodded.

Roman thought for a moment. "What's today? Sunday? I have family obligations through Thursday."

"So do we," I said. "And anyway, I'd like to get my brother-in-law in on this, as well. He's not arriving until Thursday morning."

"He's allied with Raven, isn't he?" When I nodded, he said, "All right. That's a good idea. We may need someone who can fly."

"So Friday, then?"

"Friday," he confirmed. "Pick me up at Red Rocks at eight in the morning. We can meet my contact in Cortez and get lunch, and then head to the *sipapu* from there."

"Sounds good," I said.

He nodded. "I'll see myself out." And he turned to go.

"Hang on," I said, and he turned back. I had nearly forgotten our original errand. "When you first got here, we were talking about a cure for the glamor Ingrid put on me. You said you knew a way."

"Yeah," he said, slipping back into his slacker guise. "Of course. It's stupid easy, when you think about it. Light combats darkness."

"Right," I said slowly.

"Don't you get it?" He pointed gleefully at my hair. "Our little buddy spins light. And knitting is your superpower." He waved, stepped off the bank, and vanished.

"Of course," I mumbled, as a strand of light, thin as gossamer, dropped down between my eyes. I reached into the pocket of my cargo pants for a set of double-pointed needles, and began knitting amulets.

Like all mad scientists, I tested the first one on myself. I slipped the cord over my head and dropped it into place. The bright strands flared for a moment, then winked out. "Crap," I said in dismay.

"You did it," Leonard said quietly. "It worked. The ice is melting."

He was right. The canopy of ice pellets over my timestream began to writhe, and then to drip. In moments, it was gone.

"Why are you just standing there?" Leonard said as the last of the ice dribbled away. "Knit one for me!"

When Leonard and I returned from our journey, I had the neck cords for nine amulets held tightly in one hand. Leonard was already wearing his; even though he hadn't shown any signs of the infection yet, I decided not to take chances with any of my loved ones.

Hilary was waiting for us when we awoke, so she got the first one. I kissed her as I slid it over her hair. "I hope it works for the baby, too," I whispered.

She touched her collarbone, where the necklace had flared before disappearing. "It's warm," she said. "I can still feel it."

"Good," I said, and went to hand out the rest.

Mom and Dad were next. Their expressions hardened as they realized how Ingrid had duped them.

Next was Sage. She fingered the glowing cord before slipping it over her head. "Feels good," she said as it vanished. "Does it protect against self-inflicted bad thoughts, too?"

"I'll work on one of those next," I said. Then I hefted the rest of the necklaces. "One of these is for Rafe. Do you want to hold onto it, or should I?"

She put her hand out, drew it back, and put it out again. Then she dropped her hand and said, "No. You give it to him. Some of the protection might be lost if it passes through another's hands first."

I didn't think it would, and I also didn't think it was her real reason for leaving her husband's amulet with me. But I nodded and moved on.

Grandma hadn't shown any symptoms of infection, either. "But better safe than sorry, right?" she said before putting it on. "Very nice," she said, and patted my hand.

That left me with three amulets: Rafe's, and one each for Aunt Shannon and Uncle George. I hung them in the back of the closet in my old room, under a sweatshirt that I was dead certain hadn't been washed since my senior year of high school. Even so, they lit up the interior of the closet, as well as the floor of my room just outside the crack at the bottom of the closet door.

"Is that going to bother you?" I asked Hilary, who was already in bed. "I can find another place for them."

"I doubt it. I've slept through worse. Remember that time you set up the LED installation in your office?"

"Oh. Right." That was for a different grant. I'd tried to use light to create a three-dimensional simulation of moving clouds – another of my attempts to capture something ephemeral in a manner true to its essential nature. I'd stayed up late to finish wiring it up, and hit the switch without realizing it was three in the morning.

The artist who won that grant had created a sculpture of five elephants at a watering hole, out of parts from junkyard cars.

Which reminded me of the pending grant that Hilary was so sure I'd win. Which reminded me of something else. "Did I understand you correctly earlier today?" I asked as I climbed into bed beside her.

"Which time?" She yawned and nestled against me.

"When you told Grandma we were getting married."

She froze. "Oh. That." She peered up at me. "You're not mad, are you?"

"Why would I be mad?"

"Well, because I assumed you felt the same way I do about it."

I slid my arm around her. "As it happens, I do. But you're supposed to give me the option."

She had relaxed again. "And you know this because of your vast experience with all the other women you've proposed to," she said, and stuck a finger in my side.

I flinched. "Stop it. That tickles." The light from under the closet door gave her grin an almost demonic cast. "But see, that's just it," I went on. "I'm the one who's supposed to ask."

"Is that a fact?"

"Yeah. It is."

"Well?"

"It's too late now," I said with an injured air. "We're already engaged."

She poked me again, and giggled at my reaction.

"I'm not the only ticklish person in this bed, you know," I said, and proceeded to prove it.

The tickle fight didn't last long before progressing to other things. And we did get to sleep. Eventually.

Chapter 3

I woke up ridiculously early the next morning; the glow from the amulets made the predawn darkness as bright as noon. When the bedside clock ticked over to a more-or-less decent hour, I gave up and padded downstairs to find some breakfast.

Sage was already up. "Could you guys save the gymnastics until you get home?" she said as I entered the kitchen.

"Good morning to you, too," I said. "Sorry we woke you up." And I was sorry, a little. Either she missed Rafe, or she missed the good times they'd once had, or both. I mean, I assumed there had been good times at some point. They had liked each other well enough before they moved to Washington.

"Hilary's screeching when you tickled her is what woke me up," she said. "I went back to sleep after that, so I have no idea what else you did. Nor do I care to know," she finished, forestalling me with her cereal spoon held up before her.

"You're dripping," I told her, and pulled out my own bowl and spoon as she cleaned up after herself. "Is there coffee?"

"Usual place," she said, waving vaguely toward the coffeemaker. "I didn't make any. Trying to cut back."

As I set up the coffeemaker, I asked, "Are Mom and Dad up yet?"

"Dad went for a run," she said, which is code in our family for *Dad has shifted into a coyote or something and gone out to chase prairie dogs.* "He said Mom's sleeping in. And I haven't heard from Grandma or Leonard yet." She went back to checking the headlines on her tablet.

"Anything interesting there?" I asked, as I helped myself to cereal and milk.

She didn't answer; she just kept staring at the tablet, her face getting progressively more pale.

"Sage? What is it?"

"Fuck," she said softly. "Darrell *told* me we'd gotten them all."

"All what?"

In answer, she slid the tablet across to me. I immediately saw what had upset her.

Two Dead as Neo-Atheists Clash with Police

Manassas, VA, Nov. 19 – Two men were killed and a Prince William County sheriff's deputy was wounded Sunday after police attempted to break up a protest organized by a group calling themselves the Neo-Atheist Army.

Police were called to the Manassas National Battlefield by visitor center staff, after a crowd of about 50 Neo-Atheists attempted to take over the battlefield. Witnesses said the protestors disrupted a Civil War re-enactment event, and chanted, "Everywhere, all the time," as they opened fire on police.

A spokesman for the anti-gods group said the protest was in retaliation for government attacks on Neo-Atheist facilities in Georgia and New Mexico earlier this year.

Names of the deceased have not yet been released, pending notification of next of kin. Sheriff's Department spokesman Sgt. Reece Owens identified the wounded deputy as Oscar Jenks, 28, a five-year veteran of the department. Jenks was shot in the calf and is expected to make a full recovery, Owens said.

"Those idiots," I said as I handed the tablet back to Sage. "The government had nothing to do with the New Mexico thing." I said it lightly, but the news story had sent a shiver down my back – especially the protestors' chant. Those were the same words used by Jack Rivers and Emmy Proffitt, the widow of the Neo-Atheists' founder, at the end of the group's most recent video. If *I* was chilled by the story, I couldn't begin to imagine how my sister felt. She'd been at the camp in Georgia when the JAF-H/D overran it. In fact, she had more or less started it.

"Darrell *told* me we'd gotten them all," she said again, her tone dull.

"Apparently not," I said. My cereal had gone soggy; I got up and dumped it in the sink.

"No," she said.

"Coffee?" I held out an empty mug.

She sighed. "What the hell. Sure. I'm already a jittery mess." I filled the mug and handed it to her; she wrapped her hands around it and sat back. "I wonder whether Rafe was involved in it."

My eyes widened. "You don't know?"

"We haven't talked a lot," she admitted. "It was kind of a relief when Darrell sent him off on this latest project. I felt like I could finally relax without worrying about what came out of my mouth." She looked at me. "Do you think I come off as negative?"

"In what way?" I hedged.

"Too critical. Unsupportive. Never saying a kind word, basically." She sipped her coffee and waited for my response.

I hedged again. "Is that what Rafe thinks?"

"I'm asking *you*, little brother."

"See, I don't think I'm the best person to ask," I said. "You've always been mean and rotten to me."

She blew a raspberry and sat up. "That's not what I mean. I've supported your work, right? And your relationship with Hilary?"

"Mostly."

"Oh, fine. Maybe I was a little judgy at the start. But it's just that you two are so different. I expected…"

I sat down my own mug and leaned forward. "Yes?"

She shrugged. "Someone different for you."

"Who?"

"I don't know," she said, irritated. "Just not Hilary. She was such an odd little thing — so quiet and so…*weird*. We thought she had some kind of cucumber fetish at first." *We*, in this case, meant Sage and her former best friend Kerry. My sister barked a laugh. "Then it turned out she had a kappa, which was even weirder."

I grinned. "He still eats his weight in cucumbers every few days. But we're getting off the subject."

Her smile faded. "I don't know, Webb. Rafe does think I'm too critical. But I'm trying to be supportive. It's just that my way of supporting him is to try to help him to be the best he can be. So I point out the flaws in his plans, so he can fix them — make them stronger."

"I don't think that's such a bad thing," I said. "Maybe you just need to phrase things differently."

"My therapist said the same thing." She shook her head. "But I don't know how to catch myself. I don't even realize I'm doing it until I see his expression." She winced. "I don't mean to hurt him. He's my husband. I love him. But I'm afraid…" Her voice trailed off. Finally, she said, "I'm afraid it's too late. That he'll never interpret my words the way I mean them, because he's fixated on this idea that I'm unsupportive."

I considered this. "Is he seeing a therapist, too?"

She shook her head. "He did for a little while, after the disaster in Georgia. But not now."

I opened my mouth. Closed it. Decided I might as well say it, after all. "Could it be that you're hard on him in the same way that you're hard on yourself?"

She blinked. "Am I?"

I couldn't help it — I burst into laughter. "*Are* you? Come on, Sage. For as long as I've known you, you expected yourself to be perfect."

She cocked an eyebrow at me. "Well, when people think you're going to grow up to save the world…"

I waved her off. "We're over all that. Once we got the gods moving on climate change, you were off the hook."

Her mood darkened. "Until the goddess told Mom I was supposed to have a baby on command."

"And you told Mom it's not happening. So," I said, "you're off the hook again. More coffee?" I got up to pour myself another cup.

She waved off my offer. "Yeah, but it's all of a piece, isn't it? The reaction to these ridiculous expectations gets to be ingrained after a while. I could never please the goddess. Or Mom. Not all the way." She sighed. "I should be relaxed as all hell, now that I'm a complete fuckup."

"You're not a fuckup," I said, shaking my finger at her. "You have sometimes fucked up, yes. But we all have." I softened my tone. "Perfection is unattainable. You're always going to fall short. That's one of the truisms of being human. And forgiveness is really hard – especially when the person you have to forgive is yourself."

"I don't know if I can," she said, touching the corner of one eye with her thumb. Then she got up from the table and threw her arms around my waist. "I love you."

"I love you, too," I said, hugging her back. "Now get off me, before somebody sees us and thinks we like each other."

The back door opened and Dad came in, wearing boxers in a Valentine-heart print. He froze when he saw us, his mouth a perfect O. "Uh," he said, recovering. "Good morning."

Sage stepped back in a hurry. "Hi, Dad. That's a good look for you."

"Lucky thing you had those," I said, nodding to his underwear.

He grinned at last. "I have a stash out back," he said. When Dad shifts, his clothing doesn't go with him. I've always thought of it as one of Coyote's little jokes. Anyway, if my father has to shift unexpectedly, there's always a bit of a scramble to find something for him to wear when he's ready to shift back. It has provided us with untold moments of hilarity over the years.

"Is your mother up yet?" he went on, helping himself to coffee.

"Not as far as I know," I said.

"Good. We need to talk about going after Jack." He sat at the table and sipped from his mug.

"I was thinking Friday."

He nearly choked. "Friday?" he said. "Why wait so long? We need to get this over with."

I darted a look at Sage. "Rafe wants to help."

"Well, call him and tell him to get his ass here sooner!"

"He's working on something for Darrell," Sage said.

"Then call Darrell!"

"Dad," I said.

But he wasn't about to be interrupted. "Or *I'll* call him. We need to get *going*. We've already lost too much time."

"*Dad*," I said. "There's no point in going south twice. And Roman needs until Friday to…"

"Roman?" Dad said. "Roman *Holt*? How the hell did he get involved?"

"He knows someone who can lead us to the *sipapu*," I said. "Leonard and I talked to him last night."

Mentioning Leonard had the effect I was hoping for. It was one thing for Dad to yell at his offspring, but he didn't have the same authority over Mom's cousin that he had over us. "So Leonard's okay with waiting?" he said.

"Not really," said the man himself as he joined us.

"Good morning. I'll make more coffee," I said, heading for the kitchen.

"None for me," Leonard said as he took the chair I'd just vacated, "but if you have hot water, I'd appreciate that."

"Coming right up," I said, as I filled the kettle and set it on the stove to heat.

Leonard focused on my father. "Roman barged into our meditation session last night, to be more precise. He claims to have no ties to either Loki or this Icelandic princess."

"Ingrid," I supplied.

"Who's he allied with, then?" Dad asked. "And how did he get into your meditation?"

"How he got in isn't relevant," I said, as Leonard opened his mouth to answer. I ignored my cousin's look of surprise when I said, "But he says he's allied with Hermes."

"The Greek messenger god?" Dad asked.

"And a Trickster," I said.

"Oh gods, another one," Sage groaned. "Just what we need."

I ignored her. "Roman told us Hermes used the *sipapu* to get between the gods' realm and our world after the entrance near Grandfather's wickiup was closed. He says he knows someone who can take us right to it."

Dad fidgeted with his mug. "A guide would be useful," he admitted. "Otherwise we could spend weeks checking all the kivas in the Four Corners for the one that gets us where we want to go. But Friday? When we're ready to go now?" He shook his head. "I think we're wasting time."

"I do, too," said Leonard. "What if Roman is putting us off for his own reasons? He said he had family obligations this week. Any idea what those would involve?"

I shrugged helplessly. "No. The guy just seemed to latch onto me and insist that we take him along."

Dad looked at each of us in turn. "You think we can do this without him?"

"Don't look at me," said Sage, sitting back in her chair and drawing up her knees.

"Rafe," I reminded Dad.

"Right." He turned to Sage. "Will you call him?"

Her feet hit the floor with a thud. "Fine," she said, and headed for the door to the living room.

"Sage?" Dad called.

"Yes! All right! I'm going to get my phone," she yelled over her shoulder. Then I heard her feet pounding up the stairs.

We were silent for a moment. Then Dad said, "We had a Navajo shaman on the crew a while back. George may have kept his contact information. Let me call him." He headed into the living room, taking his coffee with him.

Leonard got up to shut off the kettle. He produced a small cloth bag from the back pocket of his jeans, shook some of the contents into a mug, and poured hot water over them. "It's mint," he said. "Want some?"

"Nah, I'm good," I said.

He pocketed the bag and brought his tea to the table. When he was seated again, he said in a confidential tone, "I love Sage like a sister, but I'm glad she's not coming."

I nodded. "So am I."

Sage couldn't reach Rafe, but she called Darrell and told him what we were up to. She said before she'd even finished her explanation, he'd reassigned Rafe to us. His flight was due to arrive late that night.

Uncle George brought over Clay Notah in the afternoon. He was around Leonard's age, although his hair had not yet begun to go gray. Dad shook his hand and introduced us around. "Spider Grandmother speaks highly of you," Clay told me, as we settled into seats in the living room.

I blinked. "You've spoken with Her recently?" It had been only a month since I'd met Her, and the portals to the gods' realm had been blocked since before that.

He grinned. "A few weeks ago. She knows how to get around that Loki." He glanced at each of us. "I've been waiting to hear from you since I spoke with Her." There was a question in his voice.

"Yeah, well, we hit a snag," I said, and gave him a brief explanation about Ingrid, the glamor she'd put on us, and what we intended to do in the gods' realm.

He nodded. "I can take you to the *sipapu*," he said. "But where is your sister? I thought she would also come."

"She's not feeling up to it," said Dad. "But her husband will be coming with us. He'll be here tonight."

"He is Tlingit?" asked Clay. Dad confirmed Rafe's tribal ancestry with a nod, and Clay grunted. "All right. But Joseph, your daughter must come, too."

"Why?" Sage asked from the top of the stairs. She must have been listening to us from the upstairs hallway, which overlooked the living room. We had crouched behind the railing many times as kids to watch movies Mom and Dad didn't deem suitable for us — until Dad caught on and moved the TV to a different wall.

She came downstairs now, almost regally, as our guest stepped forward to meet her. Dad, wary, watched her as she descended. I was a little nervous myself.

She shook Clay's proffered hand, but skipped the rest of the pleasantries. "Why do I need to come with you?" she asked. "My father is right — I haven't been myself lately. Or maybe I've been too much myself." Her lips quirked up at one corner. "In any case, I don't plan to go."

Clay had retained her hand; now he patted it. "I understand. But Spider Grandmother was clear on this point. She said to tell you Cerridwen wants to see you."

For a moment, my sister's chin trembled. The Welsh goddess was Sage's protector and confidante. "All right," she said at last. "I'll go. I just hope I don't fuck everything up. Excuse me." And she stepped quickly away, through the kitchen doorway — brushing past Hilary, who looked at me with eyebrows nearly to her hairline.

I returned the look. Our simple little mission to find Freya — if you could call anything involving the gods simple — was getting more complicated by the second.

About that phone call...

Actually, I did get through to Rafe.

In fact, he picked up on the first ring. "What's wrong?"

I bristled – partly because I was still annoyed with my father, but also partly because of the implication that I never called unless it was an emergency. "Nothing's wrong. Exactly."

"Then why did you call the batphone?"

My anger deflated a little. "Oh. Did I?"

I suppose I should explain. Due to the sensitive nature of our work, we each have two lines on our phones. One is a regular number that we give out to everyone. The other is a line that's secured by as many measures and countermeasures as our crypto-technology people could come up with, and it has only two termination points – my phone and Rafe's. We can mindspeak if we're close enough, but the phone line works when we're not. It's supposed to be reserved for emergencies and mission-specific information, neither of which applied in this situation.

"I'm sorry," I went on. "I don't even know how I could have dialed it. I can call back on the other line."

"It's okay. We're here now. I can't imagine one time flouting the rules will get us fired." I could hear the smile in his voice.

"Probably not," I said, with smile of my own.

"So what's up?"

I'd meant to set up the request with an explanation first, but my own mistake – and Rafe's sweet reaction – put me off-balance. "Can you come out sooner?"

"How much sooner?"

"Tonight."

He paused – surprised, I guess – and I rushed into the silence with my belated explanation. "Dad wants to leave ASAP to find the entrance to the gods' realm, and Webb won't leave without you."

"Oh." All the warmth had dropped out of his tone.

"And I miss you," I added, very belatedly.

"I miss you, too," he said. "But you know I need to clear it with Darrell. I'm supposed to be finding the source for those memory blackouts."

"Webb knows who's doing it," I said.

"What?"

I told him about Ingrid, and the other reason we needed to get into the gods' realm ASAP.

"Well, hell. That explains everything," he said, relieved. "Let me call Darrell and check out of the hotel."

Hotel? "I thought you were still at home. Where are you?"

"Downtown." I could hear him smirking.

"Downtown *Denver?* And you didn't tell me?"

"Sage, I'm on assignment. And you're not cleared for fieldwork yet. If I stayed with you in Golden…well, I *know* you. You'd manage to get yourself involved, whether you were cleared to go back out in the field or not." Before I could respond, he said, "That's one of the things I love about you. But I don't want you to get hurt."

"I don't want to get hurt again, either," I said. "And I'm staying as far away from this trip of my brother's as I possibly can."

"Good," he said. "Let me call Darrell. I love you, sweetheart. I'll see you soon."

"I love you, too," I said, and ended the call.

I was still wiping my eyes and blowing my nose when Darrell called. I didn't want him to see me weepy, so I didn't put it up on holo.

If that surprised him, he didn't let on. "Tell me what you know," was all he said. So I went through the explanation again.

"Sounds promising," he said when I was done. "I've told Rafe he can move his operation to your parents' house tonight."

"Tonight? Why not right now?" I couldn't help but sound dismayed.

"We have evidence that the blackouts are originating from multiple sources," he said. "This Icelandic woman may have accomplices, or there may be others involved. Rafe has been working a lead related to that, and I want him to finish up before he moves."

"You don't want me helping him," I said. "That's what you mean."

Darrell sighed. "You're not cleared for fieldwork yet. You're not even cleared for full-time hours yet."

"Yes," I said coldly. "My husband reminded me of that just a few minutes ago. As if I wasn't already vividly aware."

"I know admin work isn't as interesting as being in the field," he began.

I interrupted him. "It's making me crazy! Crazier than I was to start with."

He sighed. "We've been over this, Sage. You're not crazy."

"Then let me go back to work," I said.

"I can't. Not until your counselor signs off." He paused, then tried another tack. "You know we're only doing this because we care about you."

"Yeah, yeah. Spare me." I crossed my arms.

He was silent for a long time. Then he said, "I'll level with you. I am very nervous about letting Rafe move, and you're not doing anything to ease my fears. I do *not* want you out of commission permanently. You're too valuable to the team. And the gods alone know why, but I like your style."

"Yeah?"

"Yeah. So please promise me that you won't get involved in this project of Webb's, okay?"

I ran a hand over my eyes, and sat back. "Yeah. Okay."

"And don't go along on the search for the *sipapu*, all right?"

"I *said* okay."

"Okay." Then his tone lightened. "You're on vacation, Sage. Try to enjoy yourself."

"Are you laughing at me?" I demanded.

"No, I'm laughing *with* you."

"I'm not laughing!" But I was. It was an old joke that I'd first pulled on him as a kid, when he and his wife Tess had come for a visit.

I was still laughing when I ended the call. Then I was crying again.

Darrell was right. I had no business being part of anybody's team just then.

And then Clay Notah told me Cerridwen had a message for me, but I couldn't get it unless I went through the *sipapu* to the gods' realm.

I extricated my hand from his and made an awkward exit from my parents' living room, nearly knocking Hilary down in the process. Acutely aware of the questioning looks my mother and grandmother were giving me, I hurried through the kitchen and out the back door. I had the presence of mind to step away from the house before shifting, so I wouldn't leave yet another scorch mark on the siding that Dad would have to sand away.

But after that, I didn't care about anything. All I could do was fly – and scream like a banshee to ease my jumbled emotions.

Chapter 4

Sage offered to pick up Rafe, which I totally understood. But my suspicions were aroused when she returned too quickly to have driven all the way to DIA – and neither one of them looked as if it had been a joyful reunion.

He insisted I accompany him upstairs while he stowed his suitcase in Sage's old room. I stopped first in my room to grab an amulet for him. He followed me in and firmly shut the door.

I turned from the light-filled closet, surprised. "You need something?" I asked mildly.

"Why is my wife coming along on your joyride?"

"She didn't tell you?"

"She told me. Now I want to hear it from you." Brows lowered and arms crossed, his body language added, *And this had better be good.*

I shut the closet door with the amulet cord in my hand. "Here," I said. "Put this on first."

"What's it for?" he asked. "So I'll fall for your bullshit?"

"No. So you won't fall for Ingrid's."

Grudgingly, he uncrossed his arms and put on the glowing necklace. He grunted as it winked out. "Nice job with that," he allowed.

"Thanks. Have a seat." I pointed at my desk chair, and he sat. I eased myself onto the edge of the mattress before telling what I knew. "Sage didn't want any part of this. She knows she's not ready. She even asked me to make her an amulet like the one I just gave you, but for – how did she put it?" I stopped for a moment. "'Self-inflicted bad thoughts.' That was it." I let that sink in for a few seconds. "But then the Navajo shaman who's taking us to the *sipapu* said she had to come."

"Because?"

"Because Spider Grandmother had told him that Cerridwen had a message for her, and Cerridwen was stuck in the gods' realm."

He scowled. "Convenient that Spider Grandmother could get out but Cerridwen couldn't. And convenient that Spider Grandmother couldn't just deliver the message. Don't you think?"

"If you think Spider Grandmother is leading us astray, you can unthink it right now," I told him. "I've met Her. She's the goddess who pointed me in the direction of Jack Rivers' compound. And She had a message for me from Blood Clot Boy." I heard the throb in my voice, and swallowed. Rafe had met my great-grandfather, who had been allied with the Ute creation god. He would understand the significance of that. "She's on our side, Rafe. If She says Sage needs to come with us, she needs to come. I don't care why."

Rafe shifted in his seat. It was clear my conviction had unsettled him. "But she's not ready," he said. "You said it yourself."

I nodded. "Leonard said the same thing."

"So did Darrell. He told her in no uncertain terms this morning to stay put. She'll have to act against a direct order from her superior to do what this goddess wants her to do." His anger had drained away, and for the first time I saw the concern – the fear for Sage – that lay under it. "Webb, I don't know if she's strong enough for this. She's better than she was, but weird shit still sets her off."

"Weird shit?"

"Certain smells. Leaf mold – apparently Truro shoved her face down in a pile of dead leaves when he attacked her. Pine logs and mildew." He cut a glance at me. "Sex."

"TMI," I said, waving him off with both hands.

"I know. But I'm not telling you for laughs. I need you to understand what we've been up against," he said. "What *I've* been up against." He let that sink in for a minute.

"Jesus, Rafe," I said, horrified and sympathetic at once. "I'm so sorry. Even though sorry doesn't begin to cover it."

He nodded. "Well, anyway, as I said, she's better now. And while I was glad the agency let her go back to work, she's stuck at a desk doing secretarial stuff."

I tried to envision my larger-than-life sister taking messages for some big shot. "That won't end well," I said. "She'll set fire to the desk."

"She's come pretty close to it," he confirmed, and sighed.

"Well," I said, as I propped my heels on the bed frame, "we have to take her with. We'll just have to manage her." I allowed my mouth to quirk up at the corners. "We'll be in the desert, so neither leaf mold nor mildew is liable to be a problem."

"There is that," he said. "And pine trees out here smell different than they do in the Smokies. The air is different."

"And I have no intention of having sex with her," I said, "so…"

Rafe barked a laugh. "Good to know."

"Dunno how you manage it, to be honest," I said.

His face lit up with a mischievous grin. "It's different when you're not related to her."

"I'll take your word for it," I said with a matching grin. "But seriously. We may be worried for nothing. Maybe a hike in the fresh air will be good for her."

I hadn't seen much of Mom since my arrival, but she came out of her room to see us off the next morning. "Be careful," she said, as Dad, Sage, Rafe, and I loaded up the car with camping gear and bottles of water.

Dad opened his mouth to reply. But Sage got the words out first. "We're always careful, Mom," she said, while fiddling with the straps of her daypack. Rafe, Hilary, and I laughed; my sister looked up at us, then at Dad, and then began to laugh, too.

"I have trained you well, young padawans," said Dad, above the general hilarity. Then he stepped close to Mom and gave her a long hug. "We'll be fine," he told her. "We'll be back in time for Thanksgiving dinner. Sooner."

"It's just that you're *all* going," she said, and rested her head on my father's chest.

I turned to Hilary, who had been standing at my elbow the whole time, and gathered her into my arms. "Take care of her, Hotaru," I said into her hair.

"Of course," she said. "And you: come back in one piece, hear?"

"Of course," I echoed, and held on tighter. This parting felt different than the last time I'd left her to go haring off into the desert. I'd been alone then, but less nervous, maybe because all I knew was that I had a trail to follow and a mandate to follow it. This time I had backup – but I also had a better idea of what we were up against. And more people in the party meant more to manage. Including my sister, the loose cannon.

Leonard loaded the last of the gear into Dad's SUV and looked around at the group. "We should get moving," he said. "Clay's expecting us."

"Right," I said, and reluctantly left my girlfriend's side to catch the set of keys Dad threw to me.

"Should we take more than one car?" Leonard asked. "Just to be safe."

"Not a bad idea," I said. "Who else wants to drive?"

I'll spare you the ensuing discussion. Suffice it to say that once we decided to split the party, it was clear that nobody wanted to take Sage. When I saw glints of red in her eyes, I stepped in. "We're wasting time. We have six people, so three go in one car and three in the other. I'm driving Dad's car, and we're picking up Clay because Dad's the only one who knows where he lives. So Sage and Rafe need to go with Leonard." I got in the car and slammed the door.

It took a moment, but everyone else followed suit. As Dad got in, I heard Sage say, "What the fuck, Leonard?" If he responded, I couldn't hear it; he fired up his pickup truck and backed up a little too fast, then stopped short. I backed up more smoothly and set a pace that I hoped would neither annoy Leonard further nor get us arrested for going too fast.

Dad eyed me sidelong. "What?" I said.

"You could have been more diplomatic."

"You know what was going on as well as I do."

In lieu of a reply, he entered Clay's address into the navigation system.

Clay lived in Denver, in a faux adobe house off Sixth Avenue and South Santa Fe Drive. He was out his front door and halfway to our car before I got the car stopped at the curb. He glanced back at Leonard's truck before getting into the back of Dad's car. "Trouble?" he said as he stowed his backpack on the seat beside him.

"My cousin wasn't crazy about taking my sister along," I said.

He paused, then opened the car door and got out again. He walked back toward Leonard's truck and beckoned to my cousin to get out – which he did, slamming the door with more force than necessary. Clay then took Leonard around the side of the house and out of sight.

"Now what?" Dad said, fidgeting in his seat. I caught a glimpse of amber in the depths of his eyes. If he shifted, a delay would be the least of our problems. I cut the engine and hoped Clay wouldn't take long.

He took less than five minutes. When the men reappeared, it was clear that whatever Clay had said to Leonard, it had gotten his attention. His gait was calmer, more self-possessed. And when he got in the truck, he didn't slam the door.

"What did you tell him?" I asked as Clay got back in our car.

He stared at me via the rear-view mirror and said, "The truth." He fished a crumpled piece of paper out of his back pocket and handed it to Dad.

Dad looked at what was written on the paper and began to fiddle with the GPS again.

"I don't know why I bothered asking," I said as I started the car.

We stopped at a brewpub in Durango for lunch. "How much farther?" asked Leonard as we eased into seats at a corner booth.

"Not far," said Clay as he perused the menu. "Maybe another hour to the trailhead."

"So soon?" my cousin asked. "I thought the *sipapu* was near the Grand Canyon."

Clay chuckled. "You're thinking of the Hopi *sipapu*. The Navajos came through a different hole, up in the La Plata Mountains." He went back to looking at the menu. "I think I'll have a cheeseburger."

Sage hadn't even looked at her menu. "Will we have enough light?" she asked. "Maybe we should get rooms here in town. Start fresh in the morning."

"Supposed to snow overnight," Clay said, not looking up. "Better off getting it done today."

She glanced around the table at each of us, and ducked her head to look at her menu.

After the waitress took our orders, Leonard said, "I guess I'm not familiar with the Navajo creation story, then. I thought it was similar to the Hopi."

"It is," said Clay. "We believe we're in the fourth world, although some people say we've already made it to the fifth."

His voice took on a storyteller's cadence. "First came the Black World, where the people who would become the Diné lived in eternal darkness, but with eternal life. The first people were First Man and First Woman, and Coyote, who they called First Angry. But many other people came – the Insect People, the Bee People, the Wasp People, and so on. This first world became crowded very fast, and the people sought a new home.

"So First Man, First Woman, and First Angry led them to a new world – the Blue World. There they found Blue Jay and Blue Bird, Cicada and Cricket. Wolf had a house in the east, Wildcat in the south, Kit Fox in the west, and Mountain Lion in the north. But there was still a lot of strife among the people, and it made the gods angry. They sent howling winds to destroy the Blue World. First Man devised prayer sticks with jet, turquoise, abalone, and shell, and in that way he found the route to the third world – the Yellow World.

"The boundaries of this new world were marked by the four sacred mountains of the Diné. Blanca Peak, or the White Shell

Mountain, is in the east — it's near Alamosa. Mount Taylor, the Turquoise Mountain, is in the south, near Laguna, New Mexico. In the west is the San Francisco Peaks, or the Abalone Shell Mountain, near Flagstaff, Arizona. And Mount Hesperus, or the Obsidian Mountain, is in the La Platas, just northwest of us.

"Things were going pretty well in the Yellow World until Coyote got up to some mischief." Here he glanced at Dad.

"What did He do this time?" Dad asked, although from his smirk, I had a feeling he already knew the answer.

"Stole two babies," Clay said, with such a stern expression that I half expected him to blame Dad for the ancient crime. "The babies belonged to a Water Monster, and Coyote took them and hid them. The Water Monster was so angry that he made it rain — so long and so hard that First Man told all the people to go to the top of Mount Blanca. But even that wasn't high enough to escape the flood."

"How did they escape?" asked Rafe. He seemed entranced by the story.

"They almost didn't," Clay said. "First Man planted a cedar tree at the top of the mountain, but it wasn't tall enough to reach the sky. So he planted a male reed, and it too fell short. Finally, he planted a female reed, and that female reed shot up so high that the people were able to climb up inside it and get to the Fourth World.

"Cicada was the first being to cross the boundary, and he reported it was all white and glittering."

"Snow," I said.

Clay inclined his head. "Could be. Anyway, the water kept rising until it threatened to flood the White World, too. So finally First Man talked to Water Monster to find out what he was so riled up about. At that point, Coyote admitted what He'd done and brought the babies out of hiding. He gave an offering to Water Monster in exchange for the female baby, who would be known from then on as Female Rain — the soft rain that helps the crops to grow. The male child Coyote gave back to Water Monster, and that baby became

Male Rain – the kind that comes with thunder and lightning." He nodded at Sage, who gave him a weak smile.

Our food arrived, and we spent the next few minutes eating. At last, Dad dropped his napkin on the table and said, "If we're headed for Mount Hesperus, we'd better get moving."

"Are we going to climb it?" Sage asked. "I don't think we brought the kind of technical gear we'll need. There's got to be an outfitter in town, though."

Clay shook his head. "We're not going that far. And I have everything we need in here." He hefted his backpack from the floor so we could see it. "But you're right, Joseph. We should get going."

We headed north out of Durango on U.S. 550, into the San Juan National Forest. A few miles farther on, we turned left onto a gravel fire road. The gravel petered out not long afterward, but the GPS said to keep going, so I did. The hover drive was useless here – it was a wheels-down contact sport the whole way. I spent a lot of time dodging ruts. Sometimes it worked.

I was concentrating so hard on the road that I hadn't actually looked at the GPS display in quite a while – not until Dad said, "What's that?"

I risked a glance at the device. A glowing, golden line had replaced the usual blue route marker. "That," I said, "means we're on the right track." As the SUV bounced over another rut, I muttered, "I hope."

Another half mile brought us to a slightly more civilized stretch of roadway, which dead-ended at a trailhead. And there we met a welcoming committee of sorts: my little spider buddy, and the man whose shoulder he was riding on – Roman Holt.

My stomach lurched. I probably should have told him we'd changed the date; just because he'd invited himself along on this joyride didn't mean it was fair to cut him out. But the no-decision decision not to contact him had felt like self-preservation. The last time we'd met, I'd seen a side of Roman – the steel-eyed guy – that I doubted many people got a glimpse of, and I didn't yet know what that meant. And too, I wondered how he knew to find us here.

The spider bounced in excitement as we approached, and web-swung to my shoulder as soon as I was in range. "Hey, little buddy," I said to him. "And hey to you, too," I said to Roman. "Fancy meeting you here."

"Hey, everybody," Roman said with his usual dopey grin. "I thought we weren't doing the hike 'til Friday. What happened?"

"Dad didn't want to wait," I said. "Sorry I didn't call. It's been a little hectic at our place. How'd you find us?"

He nodded at the spider, who was busying himself with something on top of my head. "He told me."

"Ah," I said, nodding, although I was more confused than ever. Was my little buddy sent by Grandmother Spider, or by Roman's god, Hermes? If the little guy was on a mission for Grandmother Spider, I felt reasonably certain he was on my side. If Hermes had sent him, he may not be – I had never met Him and didn't know enough about Him to be certain of his intent.

Or maybe he was a free agent, like Enkou. If so, all bets were off. He had helped me in the past, but that didn't mean he would continue to do so.

Dad was not very pleased to see Roman, but he was cordial to him. Sage knew him, of course; Rafe knew of him; and Leonard had met him in my head. I introduced him to Clay, who regarded him with narrowed eyes.

"We need to get going," Dad said to Clay. "We'll lose the light soon enough."

In response, Clay pulled a handful of bell-studded anklets from his pack and handed one to each of us. Interestingly, he had brought seven anklets – enough for Roman to have one, too. Was he in the habit of bringing a spare, just in case, or had he expected Roman to meet us?

I shook my head. Paranoia had never become me, and anyway, it was too late. The only way to keep Roman from coming with us would be to call off the hike for today – and Dad wasn't going to let us do that.

"This is awesome," Roman said happily as he received his bells. "I get to dance a real Navajo dance!"

Sage ignored him. "Should we be worried about bears?" she asked as she buckled the anklet.

"The bells are a warning of a different kind," Clay said, producing a hand drum from his backpack. "The entrance to the *sipapu* is hidden. We must approach it in a respectful way." He held the drum out to me. "You know how to keep a heart beat?"

"Sure," I said, and accepted the drum from him.

He turned back to the rest of the group. "I'll go first. When I begin to sing, do this." He demonstrated a dance step – toe-tap, step, toe-tap, step – that made the bells on our ankles ring, and had us all practice it for a moment. "Good," he said at last. "You guys are pow wow veterans. I can tell."

"Leonard has been a Sun Dancer," I volunteered.

"More than once," said Dad.

Clay regarded my cousin with new respect. "*Yá'át'ééh*," he said, and Leonard nodded. Lakota Sun Dancers were practically legendary for their fortitude. The dancers endured fasting and having their pectoral muscles pierced with skewers. Then they spent hours dancing under a blazing sun while dragging buffalo skulls by ropes attached to the skewers. I'd never been moved to do it, myself.

Then Clay pointed at the drum I held. "Go ahead and start. I'll lead, and you bring up the rear."

I tapped the drum with the mallet once or twice, then settled into the rhythm and began to play. Clay turned away and walked toward the trailhead, his steps in time with the beat I was setting. Leonard gestured to Roman to go next, and then followed him onto the trail, which I approved of; somebody needed to keep an eye on Roman, and Leonard was among the best equipped to do it. After Leonard was Rafe, then Sage and Dad, and then me.

We walked for maybe a quarter of an hour through a mountain meadow, its long grass yellowed and bent at odd angles. Here and there, I could see patches of snow, remnants of the storm that had taken its toll on the grass. I was warm enough, between the walk and the drumming, but every now and then a gust of wind came through that reminded me it was, in fact, late November, and we had been steadily gaining elevation.

As we approached an upslope covered in scree, Clay began his song, and one by one, we fell into the dance. As we kept moving up the slope, the air around us began to shift. It wasn't just that we were in the lee of the mountain now, although we were; the air itself smelled different. Purer. As if we had passed a boundary into another world.

Perhaps we had. For not far above us, near the crest of the ridge, I saw a cave opening that I was certain hadn't been there a few minutes before. Still dancing and singing, Clay led us into the cave.

Just inside the entrance, the floor sloped precipitously and spiraled down to the right. Clay kept going, and we followed him. The path was just wide enough for one person at a time, and a glimmer of light from the entrance gave us barely enough to see by; I wondered whether we would stop before the light petered out entirely.

At last, we found ourselves in a round, narrow chamber; the path we'd been on spiraled up the sides of the shaft. Still singing, Clay arranged us in a semicircle, with me on one end and Roman on the other. I realized belatedly that I no longer felt the golden spider atop my head; either he hadn't made the transition to this time-of-no-time with us, or he'd finished whatever he was working on up there and disappeared. I couldn't fish around in my hair to find out if he'd left me anything, though, as I was still banging Clay's drum.

He had finished his first song and now picked up another with a different melody. Reaching into his shirt pocket, he drew out a buckskin bag and sang to it for a moment. Then he opened it, removed a seed, and placed it reverently on the floor of the chamber.

He dipped once more into his backpack and drew forth a water skin, which he used to douse the seed and the surrounding dirt. Then he stepped back to a spot facing us, bowed his head, and fell silent.

I took that as my cue to stop drumming.

Breaking the silence was a tiny sound – not much more than a shiver, or the shifting of a grain of sand. I thought at first my ears were making it up. But no, it was real. And it was coming from the seed.

A moment more, and the seed coat broke with a resounding *crrack!* that made us jump. A few seconds more, and a shoot poked up from the chamber's floor. Clay began singing a different song, and encouraged me to begin playing again. Each time I banged the drum, it seemed, the little plant shot up a foot. Its base, too, widened, so that we had to step back almost to the chamber's walls to make room for it.

A distant rumble told me the plant had reached the cave's ceiling and was looking for a way through. I heard Clay stop singing – the massive plant was blocking my view of him – and then he rounded the thing and pushed us into a knot. With a knife he took from his backpack, he stabbed two diagonal slits in the enormous trunk, crossed them at the top, and wedged his knife into one side to pry the triangular-shaped piece down. As soon as Dad figured out what he was doing, he stepped up to help, and in seconds, the section of reed wall was bent out and had sagged to the ground.

"Hurry!" Clay cried, wheeling one arm toward the opening. "The ceiling's going to give way!" As if to underscore the danger, another rumble shook the chamber.

He didn't have to tell me twice. I stepped up to help the others into the reed, then dove in myself.

"Climb!" Clay yelled as he got in after me. "And keep climbing!"

I handed him back the drum, which he stowed in his pack, and began to head upwards.

The core of the reed was hollow. The outer layer was tough and fibrous, but the inner layer was surprisingly spongy. I had no trouble devising handholds and footholds wherever I needed them, and we were soon setting a good pace up the slanted surface of the reed.

A moment later, I heard what sounded like an explosion; then something began pelting our tube. I surmised the plant had broken through the crest of the mountain, and the things that sounded like hail were rocks falling through the resulting hole. One pinged off the outer wall very close to Sage's head; she cringed and screamed.

"Keep climbing!" Clay yelled.

Presently the rattling stopped, yet we continued to climb. My feet began to feel like lead weights, and my breath came in shallow gasps. Was I reaching the end of my endurance, or were we so high that we were running out of air?

A few moments later, something jarred the reed hard enough to make me cling to it for dear life. I didn't think I could go any farther. Luckily, I didn't have to.

Below me, Clay let out a breath. Then, grunting with the effort, he began to climb past me at an angle, his knife held tight in his teeth.

"Are we there?" Dad called as Clay passed him. "Are you getting us out of here?"

He nodded as he climbed past Sage.

"With that thing?" my sister said, her voice ragged with exhaustion and scorn. "Just tell me where you want the hole."

Clay stopped and eyed her, looking a little wild. Then repositioned his hands so he could take the knife out of his mouth and still hold himself steady. "Right there," he said, pointing with the tip of the knife. Then he sunk the weapon into the reed wall and sagged there, panting.

My sister shot fire from her eyes. In much less time than it had taken Clay to make the first hole in the reed down below, she had burned a rectangular portal into the wall. She tapped the top lightly, and it disappeared, making a sort of *poof* sound outside a second later.

"Everybody out," she said, and began climbing through the hole.

"First floor, shoes and lingerie," Dad intoned.

I looked at him as if he'd lost his mind. "What?"

"It's a joke," he said. "Forget it."

"Hey, that looks like snow," Roman said. For the first time, I noticed the flakes falling through the portal. "Is it snowing out there, Sage?"

"I never remember to bring my winter coat to these things," Rafe groused. "Hey, honey? Why didn't we bring our coats?"

But Sage had vaulted out. "Holy shit," she said, her voice muffled. And then a second later: "Grandfather!"

Leonard was next. "Uncle Drew?" he called in wonder, and scrambled out.

Dad and I glanced at each other and raced for the portal.

I beat him there, mainly because I was younger, and dropped from the hole into a snowdrift. I stepped away from the reed and froze.

Not literally, although it was certainly cold enough. But I stopped in mid-stride with my mouth agape at the scene before me.

We had made it to the gods' world, all right; the familiar vacant plain, ringed with distant mountains, stretched before us. But the reddish dirt I remembered from previous visits was covered with ice and snow. Blue ice and snow. A glacier.

Clearly, the weather had been wintry here for some time.

But the most shocking change was the lack of stars. All of the billions of stars I'd seen in my previous visits – each star representing a god or goddess, or so my mother claimed – were gone.

Even that wasn't the most surprising thing. For as we gathered on the edge of that familiar plain, two people faced us – people I never thought I would see again: my mother's father, Drew Sauvage, and my father's grandfather, Looks Far Guzmán.

Chapter 5

"Grandfather," Dad said, gladness in his voice. "Grandfather!"

"Joseph," said Grandfather, his voice hoarse with longing. "Do not come near me," he warned as Dad started forward. "We cannot touch you."

Dad sagged back, his eyes desolate.

"Uncle Drew," said Leonard, "it's good to see you." He almost got through it before his voice broke.

"Who are these men?" Clay asked me. I hadn't realized he had come to stand next to me.

"Our beloved dead," I said simply.

He shook his head. "They should not be here."

"No," Grandfather said. "It is you who should not be here."

"Grandfather?" Sage said. She took a tentative step toward him. "What do you mean?"

"Ah, Sage," he said. "And Webb, too. My heart breaks." He turned to Dad, his face limned in woe. "Take your children home, Joseph. There is nothing you can do here. There is nothing anyone can do. The gods are fighting one another and none will listen to reason."

"Ragnarok has begun," Grandpa Drew said quietly.

I remembered what Aunt Shannon had said, weeks before: Ragnarok would start with three years of eternal winter. Then the sun, moon, and stars would be devoured. Then the dead would come back to life. And then the gods would battle one another and the world – our world – would end. Again. And humanity would be nothing but collateral damage. As usual.

Which reminded me why we had come. I stepped forward. "We can't leave," I said. "We have to find Freya." And then I explained about my mother's illness, Ingrid, and what Loki had said.

"Where is White Buffalo Calf Pipe Woman? Why isn't She helping Naomi?" Grandfather asked. He was angrier than I'd ever seen him. "After everything we have done for Her…"

I very nearly said, *Feel free to ask Her*, but Sage spoke first. "It's my fault," she said. "The goddess told Mom that the Savior is supposed to produce an Heir, and I refused to get pregnant on Her command."

Rafe wrapped an arm around her shoulders. "And I wouldn't let her. You said it yourself, Looks Far. Sage has already done enough for the gods. We all have." Sage leaned her head against his shoulder.

Grandfather's expression darkened. "That was not part of my vision."

"What wasn't?" Dad asked.

Grandfather shook his head. "The goddess never said anything to me about an Heir. She told me of the Chosen and her team. And She said the Chosen would give birth to the Earth's Savior. But there was no mention of an Heir."

"You're sure of that?"

"I never lied to you in life, grandson," said Grandfather. "I am not about to start now."

Sage straightened in a hurry. "You mean She made it up?"

"Sage," I chided her, "She made *all* of it up." The goddess's aim had been to bring down Jehovah's reign. Centuries before, the pagan pantheons had agreed to step aside, mostly, as Jehovah brought His monotheistic religions to humanity. He had made a lot of promises about how the Earth would be better off if the gods just stepped back and let Him handle everything. In White Buffalo Calf Pipe Woman's opinion, He'd botched it – and She wasn't the only deity to think so. So She had picked Mom and Dad, along with Aunt Shannon and Jack Rivers, to convince Him to step aside.

At least, that was Her original plan. But in the end, what She got was a power-sharing agreement, with Jehovah and Jesus working alongside the other gods and goddesses to improve life on Earth. That agreement was now in jeopardy thanks to Loki – and thanks as well to whoever was behind Ingrid.

Sage flashed me a grin. We'd had this discussion numerous times – just not where anyone else could hear us. "Well, yeah. I know that.

But…" She glanced at Dad, and then at Grandfather. "That doesn't make it any easier on Mom."

"I will talk to Her," said Grandfather.

"That's great," I said, before he could tell us again to leave. "But wouldn't it be better to stop the infection at its source? We still need to see Freya."

"Absolutely not," Grandpa Drew said. "It's too dangerous."

"We are not without resources," Clay said.

Grandpa Drew frowned. "Who are you? Leonard, who are these other guys?"

Dad spoke for him. Clapping a hand on Clay's shoulder, he said, "This is Clay Notah, the Navajo shaman who guided us here."

Grandpa Drew nodded to him. "*Yá'át'ééh.*" His Navajo accent was better than mine – which could be construed as damning with faint praise, as mine was terrible. But Grandpa Drew's was really good. "And the other guy?"

"Call me Roman," said our uninvited guest, smiling. "Wow. Nice place you've got here. Is it always this cold?"

"Roman Holt," said Grandfather sternly. "You are known to us. Why are you here?"

"An excellent question," said Dad.

"What do you mean, he's known to you?" Sage asked. "Webb, what the hell are they talking about?"

All I could do was shrug and turn to Roman for an explanation.

Even before he opened his mouth, I could tell the steel-eyed man was back in charge. He stood straighter, and he met the gazes of our dead without blinking. "Gentlemen, I am here simply to assist. A great wrong has been done to Naomi. I wish to help right it."

"And what is this great wrong?" asked Grandpa Drew.

"She is being called to the Other Side before her time," he replied.

I knew it! It was all I could do to keep my mouth shut. Aunt Shannon had said Mom's doctors gave her only had a few more weeks – but I'd seen her timestream. I knew she was going to live. Now Roman was saying the same thing.

"As Webb has already explained," he went on, "my brother has fallen for a woman whose goddess wishes Naomi ill. This goddess is not Freya, but Freya knows who She is."

"Right," I chimed in. "Which is why we need to see Her."

"And there's another problem," Sage said. "There's a group calling themselves the Neo-Atheist Movement. They want to turn the clock back to the way things used to be before the Second Coming. Rafe and I tangled with them a few weeks ago." She and her husband exchanged a look; I noticed Rafe still had his arms around Sage, although it might have been for warmth as much as support. It really *was* cold on the plateau, and getting colder by the minute. "Anyway," she went on, "they've reorganized as an army, and they want the gods gone."

"Then they should be happy," said Grandpa Drew. "The gods are too busy here to meddle in human affairs right now."

"But they caught Jack Rivers!" Sage said. "He's crazy as a loon, and they're using him to get at Mom and Dad!"

At the name *Jack Rivers*, Grandfather gave Dad a shrewd look. "Where is Jack now?" he asked.

"We don't know," Sage said. "He disappeared a few weeks ago. He could be anywhere."

Grandpa Drew and Grandfather exchanged a glance. "Jack is no threat to the gods. They won't help you find him," Grandfather said.

"And Mom's cancer?" I said. "What about *that*, Grandfather? She's supposed to be forging a new agreement among the gods. They should be willing to facilitate that. They can't all want war."

"We need to speak to Freya," said Dad. "If there's a chance to save Naomi, I cannot pass it by." His voice wavered. He looked all of his seventy-four years. "Please, Drew. Please, Grandfather."

"All right," Grandfather said slowly. "But it will be extremely dangerous. Freya's demesne is in the heart of the area where the fighting is thickest. You may be wounded or killed, and there is nothing Drew or I – or anyone – can do to save you."

"I will lead them there," Roman said confidently. "They will be in no danger while they're under my aegis." He looked around the group. "Which of you is going with me?"

"I am," said Dad.

"Me, too," I said.

Rafe and Sage seemed to be having a silent discussion – or maybe a silent argument. At last, he said, "I'm coming." He strode to where the three of us were standing, leaving Sage alone and fuming.

"And what about White Buffalo Calf Pipe Woman?" my sister said harshly. "She needs to know that we've seen through Her charade. And someone needs to remind Her of Her duty to Mom!"

Another shared look between Grandfather and Grandpa Drew. "I will find Her," Grandfather said.

"I can go with you," Leonard said.

"No," said Grandfather. "Stay here with Sage and Drew. This will not take long." He turned around and trudged off, into the snow. Within five paces, he disappeared from sight.

"We won't be gone long, either," I said, although I had no idea whether that was true.

"Don't bullshit me," she snapped. "You don't have to worry about me. I won't freeze." She kicked through the snow to the massive reed stalk and slumped to a seat with her back against the reed. Presently, the area around her began to steam as the glaciated snow melted.

"Careful you don't wind up sitting in a puddle," I called.

"Go fuck yourself," she said. Then she sighed. "Be careful, you guys."

"We're always careful," Dad and I chorused.

Sage favored us with her middle finger, but she was smiling, kind of.

I'll say this for Roman: he knew how to cover ground in a hurry. The scenery around us seemed to change every few strides, from one culture's idea of the gods' realm to another. Many of these were warm and inviting.

The Norse environs, when we got there, were neither warm nor inviting.

I was reminded of my nightmares starring Ingrid as we traipsed along the icy thoroughfares. I caught glimpses, now and then, of houses where hatchet-faced people might have lived – although here, of course, the inhabitants would be gods and goddesses, and in any case none of them came out to greet us.

At some point, the golden spider returned. I hesitated now to call him my buddy, as I still wasn't clear where his true loyalties lay, and it was coloring my perception of both the spider and Roman. In any case, the little guy landed on my arm and vaulted from there to my head, where he once again began to rearrange my hair.

Maybe he was weaving me a hat. I had no way to ask him, and no time to stop and find out what was going on.

The farther we went into the heart of Asgard, the more we saw evidence of battle: churned-up earth, damaged dwellings, and sometimes spilled blood. One battlefield we crossed was huge – a mile or more wide, with a narrow creek traversing what once may have been a pleasant meadow. Now, it was unnaturally quiet; the trees and bushes were blasted stumps, and the creek's waters ran red. There were no bodies, though, and no smell of decay. Presumably the cold was keeping down the stench of death.

In the midst of one such scene of devastation, Roman slowed his pace and began to glance around. "You're not lost, are you?" Rafe called out.

"No," said our guide – the first words he'd spoken since we left the others near our arrival point. "That's it, over there." He pointed to a wooden structure the size of a barn.

"That's Folkvang?" I said in disbelief. "I thought it would be bigger. Or fancier, at least." From what I knew of Freya, She liked pretty things.

"You haven't seen the inside," Roman said, reverting to his usual guise. "Come on, let's see if She's here."

We followed Roman to the door – a massive thing, tall enough for giants to pass through without hitting their heads. He didn't bother to knock. He just pushed the door aside and walked right in.

Dad, Rafe, and I looked at each other. "I'll stay out here and keep an eye on the door," said Dad.

"And I'll do aerial reconnaissance," Rafe said. "Nobody will think a raven is out of place here." He grinned and shifted.

"Say hi to Huginn and Muginn for me," Dad said, naming Odin's raven associates. Rafe, airborne, tipped a wing in acknowledgement. "I wonder where Odin is?" Dad mused. "Maybe we could try to contact Him."

Roman poked his head out the door. "Are you coming, Webb? She's here!"

I exchanged another glance with Dad and shrugged. "Sure. Why not." And I trudged inside after him.

As soon as my eyes adjusted to the dimmer light, I realized magic had to have been involved in the hall's construction. It was many times bigger on the inside than it appeared on the outside, and beautifully appointed, with finely-crafted woodwork. But it was noisy. Tens of thousands of men and women were seated at long, beautifully-wrought tables, drinking from tankards and swapping stories of deeds past. Mead flowed like...well, like honey. Roman grabbed a couple of spare tankards from a rack on a wall and poured us libations from a pitcher at the end of the nearest table; the warriors next to it didn't appear to notice. It was as if we were wraiths – which was ironic, considering everyone in this boisterous crowd was dead.

I followed Roman to a dais upon which a golden-haired maiden reclined on a divan. A muscled warrior knelt next to Her; he held a goblet from which She took tiny sips now and then. She wore a necklace of polished chunks of amber, and a red-and-gold gown that left very little to the imagination. Several cats circled the divan, now and then rubbing up against a drop spindle that lay discarded on the floor.

I had known She was known as a goddess of love and beauty, but the spindle surprised me. "She's a goddess of spinning?" I asked Roman quietly.

"Hardly," he said with a laugh. "She practices *seidr* – the re-weaving of your destiny. Not you personally," he hastened to add.

"I got what you meant," I said.

Just then, She spotted us. "Ah! New arrivals to the hall of the honored dead!" She cried. "Please, find a seat and enjoy yourselves. You have earned it."

"You misunderstand," Roman said, all seriousness again. These personality shifts of his were disconcerting. "We are not dead. We are living humans who have come to petition You for a boon."

Freya sat up and took a better look at us. "You are Naomi Witherspoon's son," She said to me. "Thor has spoken highly of your family."

"I am," I said. "And my mother is the reason I'm here." Yet again, I explained about Ingrid and Mom's illness.

Partway through the explanation, Freya waved off the warrior. Then, as I explained that Loki had steered us in Her direction, She shook Her head. "That one has always been more trouble than He is worth," She muttered. Louder, She said, "I am sorry to tell you that you have risked much for very little gain. I do not know this Ingrid, and I am not involved with her."

"I know," I said. I'd known it as soon as I walked in the door. Freya's essence was completely different from what I'd felt in my dream. "But we thought maybe You could point us in the right direction. Maybe You can tell us who Loki's been hanging around with, or who might have the most to gain from…"

"Guys!" Rafe hissed. He finished shifting as he came through the doorway; pinfeathers resolved into fingers as he reached us. "I think I saw Her!"

"Who did you see?" Freya demanded. "And who are you?"

"My brother-in-law, Rafe Orloff," I said quickly. "Rafe, this is Freya."

"Pleased to meet You," said Rafe with a nod. Then he turned to me. "There was someone hanging around the back of the hall. It looked to me like She was trying to find a way in, or maybe She had a listening device."

"A spy," said Dad, who had followed Rafe in. "Hello, Freya. You're looking radiant as ever."

The goddess gave my father a dimpled smile. "And you, Joseph, are as gallant as ever." She heaved a dramatic sigh. "It's too bad you're married."

"Personally, I'd like to keep him that way," I said. "Do you have any idea who this spy might be, Freya?"

She tapped a forefinger against Her lips. "What did She look like?" She asked Rafe.

"Fair-haired," he said.

I snorted. "Well, that narrows it down. Pretty much everyone here is fair-haired except you, me, and Dad."

He ignored me. "She wore a gown similar to Yours," he said to Freya, "but earthier. Greens and browns. And black. And She's more…stout." He held his arms out from his body to indicate the goddess's approximate circumference.

Freya's mien darkened. "I know Her. She is Ingun, consort of My brother Frey. But why would She be in league with Loki?" She tapped Her forefinger on Her lips again, then stood. "Gentlemen, I thank you for bringing this to My attention. I shall speak with My brother, and I promise you that We will get to the bottom of this. It is very like Loki to stir the pot, but He is dabbling in the wrong one this time. Naomi must recover. We must have peace."

"Thank You," Dad said, and kissed the back of Her hand.

"Of course," said Freya, beaming. "I will send word."

"How?" I asked. "Loki's got all the exits locked down, doesn't He?"

She laughed. "Then how did all of you get in? Loki isn't as powerful as He likes to think. I will send word when I know more. And now…" She swept one hand up gracefully, and Folkvang began to fade around us.

"I can take them back!" Roman called in frustration. But it was too late – we were already back on the glacier.

I had a sense that not as much time had passed here as it had for us while we gallivanted all over the gods' realm. Grandfather had returned before us, and brought White Buffalo Calf Pipe Woman with him. Grandpa Drew and Leonard were pretty much right where they had been when we left. Clay, however, stood apart from the rest of the group.

Of my sister, the only trace was a rapidly-refreezing depression in the snow next to the giant reed.

"Where's Sage?" Dad demanded.

"Fulfilling her role in this little drama," said Clay. Except it wasn't Clay at all.

"Loki," said the goddess in disgust, as our Navajo guide transformed into the Norse Trickster before our eyes.

"What have You done with my daughter, You bastard?" Dad yelled.

"Temper, Joseph," Loki said with malicious glee. "I have waited a long time to have you and Naomi under My thumb again. I would like to savor this moment." He closed His eyes and drew in a breath.

"Your savory moment won't last long," Rafe growled, "if You don't tell us what You've done with my wife!"

"Ah," said Loki. "The husband. And the brother! Such touching devotion for a woman who's never been anything but trouble."

"The only troublesome being here is You," said the goddess, and flicked Her fingers at Him. A bubble of argent light surrounded the dismayed god. When the light winked out, Loki was gone.

I didn't think one deity could dismiss another one like that. "How did You...?" I began.

But other matters were more pressing. "Would one of you please tell me where Sage is?" Dad asked.

At once, the goddess looked contrite. "We quarreled," She said.

"Imagine that," Rafe muttered.

Leonard pointed at the reed. "She stormed up the ramp and fell through the hole."

"And none of you went after her?"

"There wasn't time," Leonard shot back. "It happened right before you showed up."

Rafe glared at him as he ran to the portal, hopped up onto the ramp – and nearly fell himself. The reed's spongy layer had turned crunchy in the cold. "Sage!" he called down the shaft. Glancing back at us, he said, "I'm going after her," and shifted. A moment later, he was gone.

"Take my clothes," Dad said to me as he shrugged out of his jacket.

"Joseph," called the goddess. Dad paused with his jacket half off. "I... I will do what I can to ease Naomi's suffering."

Dad nodded curtly and resumed undressing.

"Talk to Freya," I told Her as my father heaped his clothes on my outstretched arms. "She's going to talk to Ingun."

The goddess's eyes widened. "*Ingun?* But why is She...?"

"She's the one who's blocking Mom's recovery," I explained.

Dad, now in the shape of a falcon, cried out once and disappeared through the portal.

"*Ingun?*" She said again, thinking hard. Realization dawned on Her face; then Her nostrils flared and Her voice deepened until She was almost growling. "I will go to Freya now. Take care of your family, Webb." The edge to Her voice softened a bit. "You may find it hard to believe, with all that has happened, but I love you all."

"Believe it or not," I said with a small smile, "we love You, too."

Her expression lightened as She faded out.

"Who the hell is Ingun?" Grandpa Drew asked.

Grandfather shrugged. "Shannon would know."

"She is the ancient Norse goddess of fertility," Roman intoned. I'd nearly forgotten he was standing there. "Scandinavian kings would mate with Her to prove their fealty to the land."

"The ancient Irish kings did something similar, I think," I said. "How did She end up as Frey's consort?"

"Frey means 'lord.' One of His names is Ingunnar-Freyr – the lord of the land."

"Why would White Buffalo Calf Pipe Woman be angry with Her?" Grandfather asked.

Roman shrugged. "I have no idea."

We were all silent for a moment. Then I turned to Leonard. "Well, now what do we do? Go back down the beanstalk?" I hooked a thumb at the reed.

"We could follow White Buffalo Calf Pipe Woman," Leonard said. "Find this Ingun and deal with Her, once and for all."

I shook my head, remembering the look on the goddess's face when She promised to find Freya. "I think we can trust the goddess to take care of Ingun."

"You should go back," Grandfather said. "It is still dangerous here."

He was right, of course, but it didn't make saying goodbye any easier. "Can't you come back with us?" I said. "Mom would love to see you."

"I wish I could," he said sadly.

Leonard turned to Grandpa Drew. "Will I see you again? I have so many more questions to ask you."

"I don't know," Grandpa Drew said. "None of us knows how long this second chance will last, or how it will play out. Leonard?"

"Yeah?"

"Give your Aunt Virginia a hug for me, will you?" He laughed and wiped away a ghostly tear. "With just one arm, so she'll know it's from me."

Leonard swallowed. "Sure, I can do that."

Roman clapped each of us on the shoulder. "Let's go. I'm certain we'll all see each other again before this is through."

Where is Sage, anyway?

Nowhere good, that's for sure. Of all the wrongheaded things I've done in my life, flinging myself through that portal and back to Earth was one of the worst. If I had just kept my temper…

Wait. Let me start over.

Dad, Rafe, Webb, and Roman winked out pretty quickly. Roman must have gained more from Hermes than just his Trickster tendencies, because as far as I could tell, he was covering a lot of ground with each step.

I was kind of glad to see Rafe go. I figured he'd be safe enough – he's pretty handy all on his own, plus Dad and Webb were with him – but I was annoyed that he'd gone off to help them instead of staying with me. Sure, he'd promised my brother to help find out what was going on with Mom. Nominally, that's why we were here, after all. But still, the situation was weird and I was feeling a little shaky. Even though I just about ordered Grandpa Drew to go and find White Buffalo Calf Pipe Woman, I wasn't sure I wanted to have it out with her that very second. I wasn't sure I was capable of it. It would have been nice to have my husband there to lean on – but Rafe was set on keeping his promise. So I sat down with my back to the reed and let the heat of my anger melt the snow and ice I was sitting on.

Of course, as my little brother predicted, my ass got soaked – which made me madder still.

So I wasn't really paying attention while Leonard started babbling to Grandpa Drew, asking him all sorts of questions about Wolf Dreaming that seemed pretty esoteric to me. I got the sense they were speaking in some kind of code, since Clay and I were right there. Well, mainly because of Clay. They knew for sure that I wouldn't be able to make any use of what they were saying.

What caught my attention was the sudden silence. I looked up then, and realized time had somehow stopped. Grandpa Drew was pontificating on some point, the forefinger of his one good hand raised. Leonard was listening with a rapt expression. And Clay stood off to one side, staring at me.

"Attend, Sage!" a female voice said at my elbow. "I can only hold them for a moment."

"Cerridwen!" I began to get to my feet to greet my own personal goddess, but She pushed me back down and I scowled at Her for it. "What the hell?"

"Listen!" She hissed. "All is not what it seems. That one" – She nodded toward Clay – "is not who *he* seems. But do not let your anger get the better of you, or all will be lost."

"I don't…"

Now She was scowling. "You are not supposed to be here! The men, yes, but not you." She flicked a distasteful glance in Clay's direction.

That made me mad all over again. "Why? Because only the men can handle battle? Because only men can challenge the gods?" I barked a laugh. "Do You even know what I do for a living?"

She rolled Her eyes. "You misunderstand me," She said. "Willfully so. And there is no time to set things right. Here." She pressed something into my hand. "Keep these safe. Do not lose them!"

I opened my fist and beheld a cluster of three nuts, still shrouded in their frilly red caps, on my palm. I scowled at Her. "What am I supposed to do with them?"

"One is to plant," She said hurriedly. "The second is for your husband, and the third is for you." She glanced around. "They come! I have no more time."

"But…"

"Put them in your pocket!" She said, glaring at me.

When a goddess speaks to me in that tone of voice, I tend to do what She wants me to do. I put the nuts in my jeans pocket.

She watched me do it, and nodded once. Then Her face sagged. "Would that I…" She shook her head. "Never mind. You are here, and things will unfold as they must. But…whatever happens, My dear child, know that you are loved." She leaned over me and kissed my forehead. "They come!" She said again, and disappeared.

Time began running again. Grandpa Drew shook his finger to make his point, and Leonard immediately asked him another question. I met the challenge of Clay's stare head-on, and won. He dropped his eyes and immediately began to reorganize the stuff in his backpack.

I wondered about Cerridwen's cryptic warnings and half-spoken regrets, but I had no time to dwell on them. Two heartbeats later, Grandfather reappeared with White Buffalo Calf Pipe Woman in tow.

She looked radiant, as always, resplendent in Her white buckskin. I was somewhat less resplendent, with my jeans dripping and my soaked underwear stuck to my ass, but I stood to meet Her anyway. And as usual, I spoke first. "You lied to us," I said, my anger and frustration finding their target. "There was no prophecy about an Heir until You made it up. You drove a wedge between my mother and me, and now she's dying and You won't help her!" And to my everlasting embarrassment, I burst into tears.

"Sage," Grandfather said, trying to comfort me.

"Tell Her!" I yelled. "Somebody tell Her what it's done to us." I sank to my knees and buried my face in my hands.

"Naomi is sick?" the goddess said faintly.

"Cancer," Leonard confirmed.

"I did not know," the goddess said. "Shannon has not...?"

"Aunt Shannon can't cure her!" I said. "There's another goddess who keeps undoing everything she does!"

"Who is this other goddess?"

"They don't know," said Grandpa Drew. "Joseph and the boys have gone looking for Freya."

"And how did Freya become involved?"

I looked up, blinking away tears. "There's an Icelandic princess who's allied with Her, I think. They're trying to stop Mom from conducting the new mediation, or something." I shook my head. "I've been out of touch."

"Sage," the goddess said. She took my hand and raised me up until I stood before Her once again. "I had good reason to amend the prophecy. The situation here is dire. If We become closed off from humanity, We will need a representative on Earth."

"Like a dictator," I said.

She shook Her head, Her braids swaying. "Not at all. How could you say that? Have We dictated anything to humanity since Our return?"

She had a point. I dropped my eyes.

"And I had other reasons."

My head snapped up. "Like what?"

"I had hoped to help you and Rafe," She said, Her tone gentle.

I took it anything but gently. "You thought a *baby* would fix our marriage?"

"It's not a bad theory," said Grandpa Drew, "as theories go."

"Because Grandma being pregnant with Mom totally fixed your relationship with her," I shot back.

"If she had told me…" he said.

"It would not have mattered, Drew," Grandfather broke in. "Events would have played out much the way they did." He looked at the goddess. "Sage is right. A baby is as likely to doom a relationship as it is to save it. I saw it happen with Joseph's parents."

In a different mood, I would have pressed him for details. Neither Dad nor Grandfather had talked much about Dad's parents. But by this point, I was done with the whole conversation. "Look," I said. "I'm sure You meant well, or whatever. But I'll decide when I'm ready to have a baby. And trust me, it would be a very bad idea for us to have one now."

"Sage," She said, gliding closer to me. "Please reconsider. You don't know how important…"

"No!" I shouted, stepping back. "Stay away from me! Your job is to save my mother. Quit poking around in my womb!" I took one more step back, and stumbled against the ramp from the reed's doorway.

I don't remember climbing the ramp. But I must have, because somehow the bottom edge of the doorway caught me at the knees and I folded, overbalanced, and fell backward, screaming, right into the middle of the reed.

Over and over I tumbled, bouncing off the sides of the reed as I fell. The spongy interior cushioned me, but it also kept me from getting any sort of grip that might have slowed my descent.

Unfortunately, the root ball at the bottom wasn't nearly as spongy. The impact was enough to knock me out – and when I came to, wincing with pain, I found myself trapped inside the reed.

The doorway we had cut to get into the tube had shot up when the reed did. I couldn't even see it, it was so far above me. I guessed I was lucky that I hadn't found it the hard way during my free fall.

I groaned and checked myself as best as I was able. I was bruised and sore, but nothing appeared to be broken.

I sat back down and thought through my options. I could climb the reed again and hope it led me to the gods' realm and my family – which, sore as I was, didn't sound appealing.

My other option appeared to be burning a hole through the reed wall, hiking back to the cars, and going home. Hiking didn't sound very appealing, either, but it seemed safer than attempting the climb again.

I turned my eyes on low and cut a doorway. The chamber I emerged into was nearly dark. I felt my way up the spiral stairs and out.

A fair amount of time had passed since we'd started this crazy journey. The sun was setting and it was beginning to snow. But I estimated that I had enough time to get back to the cars before it got dark.

I don't know why I didn't just shift and fly out. I guess I wasn't thinking straight, after my argument with the goddess and my monstrous fall. And flying has never been my knee-jerk solution, anyway.

For whatever reason, I started moving on foot, back the way we had come. I had given the ankle bells back to Clay when we reached the gods' realm, and now I wished I hadn't. The noise would have helped to warn away any animals crossing my path. Lots of them come out at dusk, including predators looking for a tasty meal.

As if on cue, a low chuckling sounded in the grass behind me. It didn't sound like any animal I was familiar with. In fact, it almost sounded human.

The hair on the back of my neck stood up. I had to call on my professional training and steel myself to keep moving.

But the animal, or whatever it was, followed me. Now and again, I would hear that creepy chuckling sound – and each time, it was closer.

I breathed a sigh of relief when I reached the meadow near the trailhead. But I never made it to the cars. Something tackled me from behind. I tried to shake it off, but I tripped on an uneven patch of trail and fell headlong, whacking my forehead on a rock.

Disoriented and in pain, I tried to get up. But the thing was still on my back, holding me flat. I shivered when it chuckled in my ear. And then it spoke, and I was truly terrified.

"Little firebird," it – he – crooned in my ear. "You're a tasty morsel. Almost as tasty as Naomi. Won't she be surprised to hear Jack has her little baby girl." A filthy, gnarled hand stroked my cheek as I struggled again to get away. "Hush now," Jack Rivers said. "Hush now, *hijita*. We're going to have *such* a good time."

Pain exploded from the base of my skull, and I knew no more.

Chapter 6

The trip down through the reed took a long time, although not as long as the climb out had. The spongy inner layer was harder to negotiate going down. You could run a few paces, but then the surface itself would trip you up. After I rolled a second time, I pulled a length of cord and some carabiners from a pocket and fashioned a mountaineering line for the three of us. Leonard went first; I was second, and Roman was last.

"I hope Sage didn't roll the whole way down," said Leonard, not long after that. I pushed that mental picture from my mind and kept going.

When we passed our original entrance point, I noticed the little spider had been busy weaving a patch of shiny webbing over the hole. He jumped from the wall as we passed by and landed in my hair again. "What are you doing up there, anyway?" I asked, reaching up to try to figure out what he was doing.

"You're not fixing your hairdo now, are you?" Roman said, laughing.

"That's not..." I began, then stopped and dropped my hand. If he hadn't noticed our mutual buddy messing around on top of my head, I wasn't going to point it out to him. "You're right," I said, making a joke of it. "It won't help my looks, anyway."

On and on we walked/bounced/tripped. At last, we reached the bottom. I bent over and caught my breath; my thighs were burning from the long downhill run. "I need to get more exercise."

Leonard clapped me on the back. "Let's go," he said.

"We know your sister was here for sure," Roman said. "Wow." As I straightened, I saw what he was talking about: the doorway Sage had created was still burning around the edges. It wouldn't be long before the whole base of the reed would be compromised.

"Good thing we're all out," I said as I stepped through. "We're going to need another magic bean if we need to go back."

"There's another way in," Roman said. "I wondered what that guy was up to. Should have known it was Loki. Look – it was all a trick." He pointed back to the reed. Apparently the magic, or illusion, or whatever Clay/Loki had created had dissipated with the last of us back on Earth; we had stepped out into a meadow, not a well-shaft of a cave, and our green tunnel to the sky was nothing more than another stalk of grass.

"I bet Sage headed back to the trailhead," Leonard said. "Let's go." He unclipped the carabiner and quickly wound the line. Roman did the same with his end, and I stowed the bundle back in the same pocket.

It was dark, but the skies had cleared, and although it was too early for moonrise, starlight reflected off of the inch or so of new snow. Roman's ability to cover ground apparently didn't extend to the real world; our hike back to the cars took the usual amount of time. Leonard led, as his tracking abilities were by far the best of the three of us.

We were nearly to the cars when Leonard called us to a halt. "Look here," he said, crouching by a series of bent and broken stalks of grass. "She left the trail for some reason." He stood and pointed into the gloom. "And she was moving erratically. And there's a second set of tracks."

"Something was chasing her," I said.

Leonard trod carefully onto her path and moved along it. Roman and I traded a look and waited.

"There was a scuffle," Leonard called presently from out of the darkness.

"Do you see any scorch marks?" I called back.

"No," he said.

No? Why wouldn't she have fought back? I swallowed. "Any idea what was chasing her?" I called.

Silence for a few moments. Then I heard him tromping back. "I think it was human," he said quietly. "Bipedal, anyway."

"Sasquatch?" Roman asked with a grin.

Leonard raised an eyebrow. "We're too far south," he said, his tone serious. "And the elevation's too high for a chupacabra."

Roman's eyes widened. "Wow, Leonard. I was kidding."

"No, you *thought* you were kidding," said Leonard evenly.

"Guys," I said. "Let's focus here. Leonard, did you see any indication of where Sage might have gone after the scuffle?"

"Yeah," he said. "There's a path. But I thought I'd come back for you and Mr. Funny Guy here, so we don't get split up." He cast his gaze to the sky and looked around. "And I'd like to know where Rafe and Joseph are. It wasn't full dark when they got here."

"Doesn't matter for Dad," I said with a shrug. "He can take any number of shapes with better night vision than any of us." And then I looked at my companions and stifled a bitter laugh. Dad could shift into any shape he could think of, Leonard had the tracking ability of a wolf on the prowl, and Roman was swift of foot. All I could do was knit.

Leonard was familiar with my self-doubt; I had shared it with him plenty of times during those summers I spent with him and Grandpa Drew. Now he squeezed my shoulder and repeated what he'd often said to me: "Don't discount your talents, Webb. No one else in the family has them, and that makes you valuable beyond measure." He nodded to Roman. "Let's go."

As we followed my sister's meandering path, I felt terror wash over me. It wasn't mine; I was afraid for her, but not this way. This was the feeling of someone who was running for her life.

My steps slowed as we neared the trampled clearing. Here, the feeling of doom was overpowering; my legs crumpled under me and I landed carelessly, my hand on something sharp. I picked it up and looked at it; it was a good-sized rock, the pointed end darker than the rest. A single long hair floated away from it.

"Gods," I said. "He bashed her in the head with this." I dropped it as if it had stung me.

Roman gave me a hand up as Leonard pointed downslope. "He took a straight path from here to the trailhead. He must have carried her out." He broke into a run, and we ran after him. I don't know how we stayed upright on the uneven surface of the meadow. Maybe Roman gave our feet wings.

Only one car waited for us at the trailhead – Dad's SUV. Leonard's pickup truck was gone.

Dad came around from the other side of the SUV on four paws, with only his head human. "Took you guys long enough to get here. Son, do you have my clothes?"

"Right here," I said, and shrugged out of my backpack.

Leonard walked over to where his truck had been parked and scanned the ground. "Did you see them go?" he asked.

"Rafe did. I was a minute too late." Dad buckled his belt and slipped into his boots, then straightened. "He's tailing them. We should go."

"Where?" I asked. Everyone turned to me. "Dad, did you and Rafe agree on a meeting place?"

"No," he said, deflating a little. "There wasn't time."

"That's what I figured." I glanced eastward, where a waning moon was beginning to rise over the mountains. "Look, let's go back to Durango, get some dinner, and get rooms for the night. We can call home from there and see whether Mom or Hilary has heard anything." Fear for my girlfriend clutched at my heart. If Loki wanted to mess with me, she'd be an easy target – and she didn't have Sage's innate weaponry.

"And what if Rafe is trying to find us?" Dad said. "I need to go after him. He's no match for that bastard." Even in the starlight, I could see his eyes were wild.

"Go *where*, Dad? Rafe could be anywhere in these mountains! You'd exhaust yourself and still not find him!"

"Joseph," Leonard broke in, "which bastard? Do you know who has Sage?"

Dad sucked in a breath and willed himself to calm down. "It has to be Jack," he said. "He's probably taken her back to his trailer in New Mexico."

"No way," I said, shuddering at the memory of the interior of Jack's RV: a dark, foul midden heap, the only decoration a yellowed newspaper photo of my mother pinned above the sink. "That trailer won't hold Sage, and I'm sure he knows it. She'd burn right through it. He's crazy, but he's not stupid."

"Then where?" Dad said.

"Cheyenne Mountain," said Roman. As soon as he said it, I knew he was right. During the Cold War, the U.S. government had built what it considered to be an impregnable fortress deep inside a mountain southwest of Colorado Springs. The facility was constructed to withstand a nuclear attack. Eventually it was repurposed for other uses, and it was closed for good after the Second Coming.

"We'll need access," I said. "We'll have to contact Darrell. We should, anyway, to let him know what's going on."

"I don't want the government involved in this," my father said through clenched teeth. His eyes were glowing amber, which meant he was close to shifting involuntarily. "It will take too long for them to mobilize. I don't want that fucker's hands on my daughter!"

"Nobody wants that," I said. "We're all on the same page, Dad."

He began pulling off his clothes again. "Go ahead," he snarled. "Stand here and dawdle all night. I'm going after them."

"Oh, come on, Dad," I said, rolling my eyes.

But he was determined – or else he had no choice. A few moments later, he was airborne.

"Wow," Roman said. "I've never seen anybody strip that fast."

"Years of practice," I said as I gathered up my father's clothes and stuffed them into my backpack again. Just as I folded his jeans, I felt his cell phone buzz. I pulled it out of his pocket and discovered a message was waiting from Hilary.

I checked my own phone; sure enough, she'd sent the same message to me – and to Rafe, not that he would be retrieving it any time soon. The message consisted of a video file. "This can't be good," I muttered as the others gathered to watch over my shoulder.

It wasn't.

It was less than ten seconds long. Jack Rivers peered into the camera lens, a maniacal grin on his face. "Naomi," he breathed, then cackled. "Look who I found!" He trained the phone's lens on a familiar figure: my sister, out cold, and slumped into the passenger seat of Leonard's pickup truck. The camera panned back to Jack. "She could have been mine, you know. But you slept with Joseph instead of me." He nearly spat my father's name. "But that means it wouldn't be incest if I did all the things to her that I wanted to do to you. Remember?" He licked his lips and growled deep in his throat. Then the maniacal grin was back. "There's only one way you can stop me, Naomi. Come to me. Come to me, and I'll let her go."

"Fucker," Leonard said under his breath.

"Yeah," I said while I messaged Hilary: *Where did this come from?*

He sent it from Sage's phone to your mom just now. She's pretty upset.

I could only imagine Mom's reaction when she opened what she'd thought was a message from Sage and saw that maniac's face instead.

Where are you guys? Hilary messaged again.

Near Durango. We got to the gods' realm. Freya's on notice, and the goddess says She'll help Mom. How is she?

The same.

I wanted to howl in frustration. Everything was either moving too fast or not fast enough.

Tell Mom Rafe is on Jack's tail. We think he's heading for Cheyenne Mountain. That's where we're going, too.

Be careful. I love you.

I love you too. I didn't have the heart for the usual flippant response; if we'd been careful, I thought, we might not be in this fix at all right now.

But I knew better than to pursue that train of thought. Being careful only ever got you so far when the gods were involved.

"Coming?" Leonard called from the passenger side of the SUV. He and Roman were waiting for me to unlock the doors.

"Yeah," I said. I pocketed my phone and caught up the backpack by one strap. I wasn't sure who was running the show now – whether Loki was in charge, or whether He'd cut Rivers loose to be a free agent – but regardless, I was going to have to see it through to the end.

Chapter 7

We got takeout at a fast-food place in Durango, at Roman's insistence, and got back in the car. Roman was the only one hungry; I think Leonard took one bite of his burger and shoved it back in the bag. I munched on fries without tasting them as I drove.

Hovering, and selective adherence to the speed limit, got us to the Springs in a couple of hours. The moon was high in the sky by the time we reached the main gate into the Cheyenne Mountain Complex.

"I thought this place was abandoned," Leonard said as we crept forward to a guard shack that was well-lit and very much in use.

"Me, too," I said. I was sure I'd seen a fairly recent photo of the facility in which the gate was securely locked, with a sign saying **NO TRESPASSING BY ORDER OF THE U.S. GOVERNMENT** in big, friendly letters. I pointed at the doorway to the guard shack. "And that guy doesn't look like a member of the military to me."

"I'll handle it," Roman said in his ultra-serious voice.

"Okay," I said with a shrug, and rolled down my window.

The guard was well-appointed, with a helmet and flak jacket, and some sort of automatic weapon – Sage or Rafe would probably know what kind – held at the ready, in case we had no business being there. Which, of course, we didn't. "State your name and business," he said.

Roman leaned across me and intoned, "We have a message of the utmost importance for your commanding officer."

I nodded to the guard with as much sincerity as I could muster.

"I'll take it," the guard said.

"No. We must deliver it in person," Roman said.

"By whose order?"

"By order of High Commander Price," Roman said.

The guard considered that. "One moment," he said, and backed a few steps away from us to say something into the mic strapped to his upper arm. I couldn't hear what he said, and I also couldn't hear the substance of the response. "Copy that," he said into the mic as he walked back to the car. "You are not on the security checklist," he said to Roman. "We have not been told to expect anyone tonight."

"I am not surprised," Roman said. "It's an emergency situation. Code Crimson."

The guard's face paled. "Password?" he barked.

"Emmeline," said Roman.

The guard waved us through.

Once inside the gate and outside the range of its floodlights, Leonard grabbed Roman's shoulder. "Just who the hell are you?" Leonard demanded. "Who are these people, and how did you know the password to get us in?"

"If you quit manhandling me, I'll tell you," Roman said, shrugging free of my cousin's grip. "Ow." He massaged his shoulder for a moment. "These guys are Neo-Atheists. I recognized the insignia on his collar."

If that were true, I worried even more about Sage. This would be the second time she'd fallen into their hands, and the first time didn't end well. Assuming Rivers was still working with them, that is.

"And the password?" I prompted.

"My father used to be the President," he said. "He still gets security briefings. Sometimes I listen in."

"We need to tell Darrell," I muttered.

"You mean Darrell Warren?" Roman asked. "He already knows."

"What?" I cried, jerking my head around to look at Roman.

"Hey there, careful," he said, grabbing the steering wheel. "You'll run us off the side of the mountain."

I swung my gaze back to the narrow, winding road. Roman wasn't wrong about the possible effects of my inattention. "How do you know Darrell already knows?" I said.

"Because he's the person who briefed my father."

Mentally, I clicked through a number of associations in rapid succession. "And Rafe was on the team that was assigned to check it out," I said. "Wasn't he?"

"A gold star for you," Roman said in an approving voice.

"No wonder Darrell didn't want Sage going along," I mused. I pulled into the parking lot and cut the engine. A few vehicles were parked in the lot, but Leonard's truck wasn't among them. I wondered if that meant we had guessed wrong about where Jack was headed. But no – it made too much sense. He needed to stow my sister somewhere that she would have trouble getting out of. Cheyenne Mountain fit the bill in too many obvious ways.

I turned to Roman. "Well, we're here. Now what?"

"We go in and find High Commander Price," Roman said, "and tell him that the JAF-H/D agent who gave his people so much trouble in Georgia is somewhere inside his complex. Then we let them find her."

I stared at him. "That is a spectacularly bad idea," I said. "They'll kill her."

"Maybe Rafe has already found her," Leonard said. "Do we have a way to contact him? Let him know we're here?"

"Sage could," I said, raising my hands in a helpless gesture. "We don't know where Dad is, either."

"They're going to expect us to go in," Roman said, glancing toward the tunnel. "I suggest we head on up to the entrance and play it by ear."

I unbuckled my seat belt. "Well, that strategy has gotten us this far," I said, and piled out.

The guys at this guard shack let us through, as well. A long hike brought us to the famous tunnel and its massive blast doors; on the other side of them, I saw the Neo-Atheists' logo prominently displayed on banners that covered any mention of the facility's former owner-operators.

"Which way is the stargate?" Leonard muttered.

"What?" I turned to him.

"It's from a TV show my father used to watch," he said. "Never mind. Roman, where are we going?"

We had stopped at the intersection of a number of tunnels. Some of them appeared to lead deeper into the complex. One to our left was marked as the way to the village – the homes and entertainment facilities where the crew and their families had lived, back when Cheyenne Mountain was a working military base. Another was designated as the way to the south portal.

"There's another entrance?" I asked.

"Yeah," said Leonard. "It was used more or less as a loading dock."

"Maybe that's the way Jack came in," I said. "That would explain why your truck wasn't in the parking lot."

"You guys," Roman said, "we need to go see the high commander."

"I thought that was just a ruse to get us in here," I said. "Do you actually have a message for him?"

"They're going to expect us to go to that office," Roman insisted. "Once we're done there, we can find your sister."

"You *do* have a message for him. Roman, who are you working for?"

"Not *for*," he said. "*With*. This way." He strode confidently to the middle passageway and disappeared down it.

Leonard and I exchanged a shrug, and followed him. As we hurried to catch up, I hoped somebody else was closer to springing Sage than we appeared to be.

While Webb was following Roman...

I came to in the dark.

I groaned and began to sit up, and then thought better of it. My head hurt like a son of a bitch, and my whole body felt bruised, as if I'd fallen down a flight of stairs.

Or the inside of a reed. All the way down from the gods' realm.

The day's events were beginning to come back to me. My argument with White Buffalo Calf Pipe Woman. My long, long fall to Earth. My terrifying flight from some unknown entity, and then my capture by the loathsome creature who had called me *hijita*. Little daughter.

I suppose in some sick and twisted alternate universe, I could have been Jack Rivers' daughter. Maybe there, he would have defeated my father – killed him, even – and won my mother's heart. Or maybe he would have raped Mom for real, and Dad would have manned up and raised me as his own.

But we didn't live in that universe. We lived in this one. And in our universe, Dad was my father – my real, biological father – and Jack Rivers was a crazy old coot who still had a thing for my mother. Even though she was over seventy and dying of cancer.

Well, maybe not dying any more, if the goddess had actually listened to me.

My JAF-H/D training kicked in as I assessed my surroundings. I was lying on an unyielding surface – linoleum over concrete, maybe? The air didn't smell stale, so there had to be some type of ventilation in whatever chamber I was in. And ventilation meant there was a way out.

I pushed myself up more slowly this time, pausing when I began to feel dizzy and waiting until the sensation passed before trying again. It took several minutes for me to achieve upright status. At that point, I ignited my eyes – on a very low setting, in case someone was monitoring my movements.

I was on the floor of what appeared to be a control room. The room was long and narrow with a solid door at one of the ends and a counter along the length of one side. I couldn't see over the lip of the counter from my spot on the floor, but I assumed there would be monitoring equipment – computer screens and meters – on top of it.

I was right about the ventilation. There was an intake vent in one corner and an outflow vent in the opposite one. Both were near the ceiling and neither was large enough for me to fit through it.

I slid my butt along the floor to the door at one narrow end of the room and tried the handle. Locked, of course, and with no key in the keyhole. I presumed it was locked from the outside. With a bobby pin and a little time, I could have picked the lock. But I needed to be on my feet first, so I could run once the door was open.

The door handle and the adjacent counter gave me two points of leverage. I sucked in a breath and heaved myself to my feet. Then I braced myself against the counter until the pounding in my head passed. It took some time.

When I thought I could open my eyes without screaming, I gave it a try.

Sure enough, the counter supported a number of monitors, gauges, and switches. There was also a window that ran almost the entire length of the room, and on the other side of the glass I beheld two things: several pools of water, long and wide, and carved from the living rock – a reservoir or heat sink or both; and Hilary's kappa, Enkou, who was waving madly at me from the side of the nearest pool.

It was only then that I deciphered a sound that I'd been hearing since I came to: the *drip drip drip* of water coming in where it's not supposed to be.

Carefully, I turned my head toward the sound. There, in the far corner, under the counter, I saw it: a tiny crack in the wall and a puddle forming under it.

I shot Enkou a thumbs-up and moved slowly toward the puddle, keeping my head as level as possible and using the counter for support. Then I sank to the floor again and contemplated the salvation Enkou had devised for me. I cupped my hand under the crack and caught a few drops in my palm. It wasn't enough for a real drink of water, but I licked them up anyway.

The water droplets in my palm reminded me of something else I'd recently held. I slid my hand into the pocket of my jeans and pulled out the gift Cerridwen had given me in the gods' realm. One of the nuts slid out of its battered red cap and landed squarely on my palm. *One is to plant*, She had said. I looked dubiously at the floor where the puddle was forming – I hadn't been wrong about either the linoleum or the concrete – but I figured it was worth a try. With shaking fingers, I dropped the nut into the puddle, and returned the others to my pocket.

At that moment, I heard the sound of a key in the lock. I doused my eyes just as the door banged open. My crazed captor stood silhouetted in the doorway. "*Hijita*," he crooned. "You're awake. *Qué bueno*." He flipped a light switch on the wall, and neon lights on the ceiling stuttered on. Then he shut the door and pocketed the key.

"Stay away from me," I said as he advanced toward me. "And don't call me your daughter. My father is Joseph Curtis."

He hawked and spat, the sputum landing barely an inch from where my hand rested on the floor. "Do not mention his name to me! That *cabrón* isn't fit to lick Naomi's boots!"

"Nevertheless," I continued sweetly, "he has very likely licked many interesting places of hers that you have not."

For a moment, I truly thought his head would explode. Then his eyes narrowed. "Would you like to know how I have licked her?" He ran his tongue suggestively over his lips.

"Thanks, but no," I said, scooting away from him, careful to keep between the puddle and my captor. The sudden movement caused my head to begin pounding again.

"But yes," he growled, shoving his face close to mine. As I flinched away, he took the neck of my t-shirt in both hands and ripped until it gaped open, exposing my bra. "Such small *chichis*. Your mother's are bigger," he said. Then he bent over them and began to lick my chest along the top edges of my bra. I squirmed. One of his hands caught me fast at the small of my back, while the other reached behind me for the bra clasp.

"Yeah, well, I'm taller," I said. His hair, where it brushed my chin, was stiff with dirt. He smelled as if he hadn't bathed in a year. I wished for my head to stop hurting so I could fire up my eyes and fry every last disgusting hair from his filthy head.

He froze. It wasn't anything I'd done – I was sure of that. But then something cool and green caressed my forehead. A leaf?

I risked a glance upward. It was, in fact, a leaf – bright green and growing from a fairly substantial branch. And its touch had cleared my head of pain.

Then I heard the sound that had made Rivers pause in his mauling of me – a soft *crrack!* As if something was giving way. A wall, maybe, or the floor we were sitting on.

"*¡Hijo de puta!*" he said under his breath, backing away from me. His eyes had widened. "There's a *tree* behind you!"

I smiled. With a groan, the base of the counter shifted away at an odd angle, and I felt a substantial breeze at my backside. I guessed the taproot had drilled through however many layers of metal and concrete shielded the room to get to the watery bonanza in the reservoir below.

The building groaned again as part of the floor began to tilt. "Adios, asshole," I said, and wiggled through the hole Cerridwen's tree had made in the wall behind me.

I heard a familiar croak overhead, and my heart soared. Heedless of my wounds and indignities, I shifted and joined my husband in flight above the reservoirs. I circled once – a victory lap, and a mistake. For Jack Rivers had a gun. It went off, and a new, fiery pain blossomed in my side – one that had nothing to do with my own flames. I faltered and fell, plummeting into the reservoir below me, and knew no more.

Chapter 8

Roman seemed to know where he was going. Leonard and I followed a short distance behind him as he walked to a stairwell, opened the fire door, and headed up.

Leonard caught the door before it closed and held it open for me. Together, we began mounting the stairs.

After the first two flights, I began to lag behind. I'd already done more physical exertion that day than I usually did in a week. Leonard had a couple of decades on me, but he spent much of his life outdoors and was in better shape. Apparently Roman was part gazelle.

At last, I stopped on a landing. "Go ahead," I wheezed in Leonard's general direction. "I'll catch up."

He nodded and sped up the stairs after Roman. Groaning, I heaved myself upward at a more sedate pace.

I lost sight of them, of course. But I recognized Leonard's bandanna knotted around the banister on the fourteenth floor. I sucked in a breath, untied the knot, and stuffed the bandanna in my pocket. Then I opened the fire door and plunged through it.

I don't know what I expected to find on the other side. Chaos, maybe. Fire, pestilence, and flood, at the very least. Instead, I found myself in a cinder-block-walled hallway lined with doors. I'd expected hell, and found an office suite. Which might be the same thing, depending on who you ask.

I heard voices to my left. A door was open at the end of the hall, so I made for it – but as I approached, I slowed. Maybe it would be better for all of us, I thought, if I stayed out here and played backup. Not that I had any weapons to speak of, other than yarn and my devastating wit, but at least I could act as a lookout. So I parked myself up against the wall next to the open door.

"I need to see the high commander," Roman said, and clearly it was not the first time he'd said it.

"You cannot see the high commander without an appointment," a matronly voice said in a dispassionate tone.

I blinked. Had we been up all night? Or did the high commander have staff outside his inner sanctum at all hours of the day and night?

I risked a glance around the doorjamb and saw Roman addressing a computer terminal – the old-fashioned kind with a physical keyboard and a little camera gizmo. The screen was pointed toward me, but the disapproving woman whose face glared out of it was focused on Roman, and took no notice of me. She might not have even realized Leonard was also in the room; he prowled along the back wall as if tracking something. That's when I realized she was probably a bot.

Still, we might need the element of surprise, or something. I pulled back from the doorway and trained my eyes on the hall, while keeping an ear toward Roman's efforts to get past the high commander's secretary.

"Then I would like to make an appointment to see the high commander," Roman said, putting every ounce of authority he could muster into his tone.

"Certainly. When would be convenient for you?"

"Right. Now."

"I'm sorry," the bot said, "but the high commander is not available at this time. Perhaps you would like to come back next week? Tuesday is clear."

"This is an emergency," said Roman. "Tuesday will be too late. By then, the Earth will be lost." His tone darkened. "Unless that's what the high commander wants."

I blinked. The Earth would be lost by Tuesday?

"Oh, enough," said a new female voice – this one richer and more immediate than the bot's. Without thinking, I looked into the office again.

A woman stood between Roman and the computer terminal. She was voluptuous, with the fairest hair and the bluest eyes I had ever seen; happily matched as I was with Hilary, my heart ached to behold her. She wore camouflage – greens, browns, grays and black – in a flattering cut that was in no way standard issue, with a Neo-Atheists patch on her shoulder and several pips sewn to the collar of her shirt. But when she moved, her clothing shimmered oddly. I frowned, then adjusted my sight and looked again; her pants and tunic morphed into a figure-revealing gown in the same shades as her uniform.

Not her uniform; *Her* uniform. The camouflage was a nice touch for a goddess hiding in plain sight.

I stepped into the room. "White Buffalo Calf Pipe Woman is looking for You."

She turned to me. "No doubt. But She will never find Me here." She laughed. "Loki has promised not to let Her out of His sight. You're Webb Curtis, aren't you?"

I inclined my head. "Guilty as charged."

"Loki told Me about you. It seems you pulled one over on Him." She laughed again. "He was angry about it for days."

"No doubt," I echoed. "So You're in charge of the Neo-Atheist Movement? That doesn't say much for Your self-esteem."

"Oh?" She said with a tiny frown. "How so?"

"You're encouraging a bunch of humans who want the gods to go away. They would destroy You if they could." I shrugged. "You're sowing the seeds of Your own destruction."

"And?"

I blinked. "That doesn't bother You?"

"My dear man, it's My purpose," She said loftily.

I glanced at Roman in confusion. "I thought You were a fertility goddess," I said.

"Yes, of course. But not in the sense you mean." She glided closer to me and began to unzip my jacket. "The sex act is pleasurable. But it's pleasurable for a reason." She caressed my chest with Her palms. "It culminates in the act of creation." She watched my face as Her hands moved farther down. "You want to have sex with Me, don't you? Oh, yes, you do. You can't hide anything from Me."

Of course I did. She was beyond beautiful, and I was ready. She had made me so.

She slid Her hands to my buttocks and cupped them, snugging me up against Her. I swore I could feel Her nipples pushing into my chest. My hands, which I hand been holding resolutely at my sides, rose of their own volition; my thumbs slid between us, reaching for those maddening points of Hers.

"Yes," She crooned, rocking Her pelvis slightly against me. "Oh, yes. I can almost feel you in Me. You can feel it, too, can't you?"

I could. A groan escaped me as my thumbs reached Her nipples at last.

"Oh, that's nice," She sighed, and unbuttoned my pants. "I could take you right here, in front of your friends."

Belatedly, I remembered we had an audience. I forced my hands away from those luscious breasts and tried to pull away.

"Oh, no, little spider," She whispered. She grabbed my butt again and forced me to look at Her. Even as She continued to push against me – even as my body responded, whether I wanted it to or not – Her lustful smile turned to a sneer. "You aren't going anywhere. For the flip side of creation is destruction, and I mean to destroy you."

"No," I breathed, as She forced me against the wall and fixed Her mouth on mine. I felt my pants slide to my ankles. Her dress disappeared; there was nothing between us. All I had to do was aim true…

"Get off of him!" Leonard roared, yanking Her by the shoulders with both hands. Panting, I opened my eyes. What the hell? We were both fully dressed. My jacket was still zipped, even. But my lips felt bruised, and I had the hard-on to end all hard-ons.

"Would you like the same treatment, Wolf Dreamer?" She purred, reaching for his butt. "I've always wondered what White Buffalo Calf Pipe Woman saw in Coyote. Maybe you and your Wolf friend could show Me." Her teeth nipped at his lower lip, and fastened on.

"Let him go!" I howled.

Still locked in an embrace with my cousin, She threw me a beckoning look. "Oh, this is rich. Should we make it a threesome?" She ground Her hips against Leonard's crotch. "Or should I let you fight over Me?"

"Ingun, that's enough," Roman said, his gaze razor sharp.

"Oh, all right," She said with a sigh, and let go of Leonard. "Spoilsport. You and your mother are two of a kind." With a last, longing look at both Leonard and me, She straightened the collar of Her uniform and turned to Roman. "You said you had a message for Me. Deliver it and begone."

"It is this," he said. "It's over. The other gods are on to You and Loki. They will not let this charade You are calling Ragnarok continue."

"Charade?" She said, and laughed. "My dear little man, it is no charade. The realm is in the grip of winter, is it not? The dead have returned. The Giants have come. The battle has already begun! How can you call it a charade?"

"Because it is not yet time, as well You know," Roman said. "Loki persuaded You to start the clock too early. Millennia were to pass before Ragnarok came again – but You were angry when White Buffalo Calf Pipe Woman agreed to share power with Jehovah. You thought You deserved a bigger role."

"I deserve to be in charge!" She cried, and the floor wobbled a little. "That prissy little New World upstart insinuated Herself into the process *I* began. I wanted Jehovah *gone*."

"You wanted to end the world," Roman said.

"I wanted My life back!" She shouted, and the room rocked again. I wondered briefly if it was a localized phenomenon or whether She was truly rocking the building. If it was the latter, it was an impressive move. After all, the complex had been built to withstand a nuclear blast.

But a bombing would be an external event. I wondered what effect an explosion *inside* the facility would have.

The odds were good that we were going to find out, as Ingun was still raving. "That upstart Freya stole all my followers and divided them up between Herself and Frigg. And then She styled Herself a love goddess." Ingun sniffed imperiously. "Ha! That childish creature wouldn't know love if it bit Her. It's all sex and petty baubles to Her. She has *never* understood its true power."

"Pain," I said. "You believe love's true power is pain. Manipulation. Gaslighting. Abuse and control."

She grinned fiercely. "All that, and more. I knew you would understand, little spider."

"But You're wrong," I said. "Those aren't manifestations of love. They're perversions of it. They're...destructive."

"Now you're catching on." She took another step toward me. A scant foot separated us. "I am the mistress of Creation and Destruction. I am the mistress of Love and Hate."

"But hate isn't the opposite of love," I said. "The opposite of love is indifference."

She paused, Her mouth agape.

"Now," Roman said quietly. And from the top of my head, a shimmering net, woven finer than anything I could have produced, sailed through the air and wrapped tightly around Her.

She cried out and fell to the floor, struggling against Her silken bonds.

"As I said, it's over." Roman stepped toward me as the golden spider scampered down my arm. "Nice work," he said, and high-fived the little guy. Then he high-fived me. "You, too. You're amazingly cool under pressure."

I laughed shakily. My crotch wasn't quite yet back to normal. "Yeah, thanks. What do we do with Her?"

Roman considered the shrieking cocoon. "She'll be okay here for now," he decided. "We need Her to get to Loki. But first, we need to find your sister." He clapped me on the shoulder and headed toward the stairwell.

"Uh, Roman?" I said. "Does this place have elevators?" I was pretty sure I wasn't going to survive another climb, either up or down.

"Oh," he said, a grin overspreading his face. "Yeah, it does. This way."

As we rode the elevator down to the first floor, I said, "I've got a question for you."

"Shoot," Roman said.

"How come Ingun came on to Leonard and me, but not to you?"

He threw back his head and laughed. Then, seeing my mystified look, he said, "Come on, Webb, think. Ingun has no power over a man who's not attracted to Her."

"Oh. But…? *Oh.*" I thought about all the years I had known him, and realized that while I'd often seen him with women, it never seemed serious, or even romantic. On the other hand, I'd never seen him with a man – but there may have been good reason for that. "Do your parents know?"

"Yeah."

"Are they okay with it?"

"Mom is."

Well, that answered that.

Roman side-eyed my cousin with a smirk. "Relax, Leonard. You're too old for me."

"You're not my type, either," he said. "And before you ask, Webb, no, I'm not. Just never found the right girl."

"Woman," I corrected.

"Woman. Right." He flashed me a smile.

The elevator doors opened onto an empty corridor. "I wonder where the rest of the crew is," I said as we walked toward the exit.

"My guess is they don't have enough recruits yet to staff this whole place," said Leonard. "We may not see anyone at all unless we run across their operations center. Or at shift change."

"And who knows when that will be," I said.

"I know the JAF-H/D mission in Georgia hurt their recruitment efforts," Roman said. "And knocking out that transmission center in New Mexico was another blow."

Once again, I was struck by how much Roman knew. "Hey, Roman? That message you gave Ingun – who was it from?"

"My mom," he said.

I slowed for a moment as I digested that bit of information. "Not Diana," I said. The former First Lady was allied with the Roman goddess of the hunt.

"Nope," he said. "This came straight from Mom. She finally got Dad to tell her what Loki and Ingun were up to, and she just lit up."

"I can imagine."

"She's been trying to contact Diana ever since, but of course the transmission lines are down, as you know. So she asked me to see if I could get a message through."

"She knows you're allied with Hermes, then."

He snorted. "She could hardly avoid knowing, after wingéd Mercury landed one night in the Rose Garden. The Secret Service was *not* amused."

We passed out of the building and into the main corridor of the complex; I could see the tunnel entrance from where we stood, and the darkness past the lights from the parking lot. "Which way?" I said.

A raven dive-bombed us, croaking in relief. "Rafe!" I called as he landed and shifted.

"There you are," he said. "I've been looking all over for you."

"Where's Sage?" I asked. "Did you find her?"

"Rivers has her. And she's hurt."

"Hurt?" I said, remembering the bloody rock I'd touched in the meadow.

He gritted his teeth. "It was my fault. She was free of him. I was guiding her toward the exit, but she took a victory lap around the reservoir enclosure, and he shot her."

"What?" A mental picture intruded of my sister bleeding out somewhere. I pushed it away. "Where is she? Where's Rivers?"

"She fell into one of the reservoirs. I knocked him out and threw the gun in the water, and then dove in after her – but I couldn't find her." He gritted his teeth in frustration. "He was still out cold when I surfaced. So I came to find you guys."

"The reservoir is this way," Roman said, pointing. "Let's go. Maybe we can track them down."

"On it," said Leonard, taking the hallway at a run. The rest of us were right behind him.

And now we pause for a peaceful interlude.

Considering I'd been whacked on the head twice, shot, and sexually assaulted *again* – not to mention beat up from my tumble down the reed – I awoke feeling better than I had any right to feel.

I raised my head carefully and looked at my surroundings. I was lying on the grassy bank of a stream that I didn't recognize, although it seemed familiar. Comforting, even. The lush grass didn't extend far from the water's edge. Past it was a shortgrass prairie of the sort we used to be able to see from the cliff where Grandfather's wickiup had stood.

Thinking of Grandfather gave me a pang. It had been amazing to see him in the gods' realm, and now I missed him all over again. I wondered whether Roman was right that we would all see each other again before this was over.

Now and again, a *squish-thump* interrupted the soothing burble of the stream. I turned my head and saw Enkou, of all things. Hilary's ninja turtle was building up the berm – filling his flippers with mud from the stream bank and plopping it atop a ridge. The berm's sides were beginning to curve in toward the middle of the channel. It was clear to me that he intended for them to meet in the middle and form a catchment pond.

"Expecting a flood?" I called.

He grunted and went on with his work.

I didn't have a degree in environmental engineering for nothing. "That's going to wash away, you know. It needs an internal support structure – branches or something – for the mud to adhere to." I looked around, but the area was devoid of anything that would fit the bill. There weren't even any trees to uproot.

"Does not need to last for long," he said.

I tried to turn so I could see him better, but hissed as the movement awakened a burning pain in my right side. My hand went to where the pain was, and discovered someone had packed mud on an area that extended from my lowest rib to the top of my hipbone, and from my navel to my back. "What the hell?"

"No touching," Enkou said, slapping my hand away with a muddy flipper. "Poultice."

"Poultice?" I looked at the mud again, and then at Enkou. "You're trying to draw the bullet out of me, aren't you?"

"No time for doctor," he said. "Nowhere to go. Bad man would have had Sage again."

Bad man would have… I shivered. "Well, thank you for rescuing me."

He grunted again and went back to his construction project.

"Enkou?" I asked presently. "Where are we?"

"Webb's head."

"What?" That time I did jerk around to look at him, and my wound immediately reminded me how bad an idea it was. "*Fuck*," I hissed. "We're inside my brother's *brain?*" Then I remembered something Webb had said about the way he did business – something about constructing a simulation of the timestream in his head. "We're in his simulation, aren't we?" I looked around again. "Whose timestream is this? Mine?" It didn't look like anything I would have cooked up.

"Joseph's," Enkou said.

That explained why it felt so comfortable. "Okay, but why are you building a catchment pond in my father's timestream?"

"Not catchment pond," he said. "Weir."

"Right," I said, rolling my eyes. "Look, what's this all about?"

"Told Webb already," Enkou said. *Squish-thump.* "Protect against darkness."

Great. As if things weren't already weird enough, apparently now the Big Darkness was gunning for us. Or for Dad, at least. Whatever the hell the Big Darkness was.

Then I thought of something else. "Hey, Enkou? You didn't bring my body here, right? I mean, I'm not physically inside my brother's head. Right?"

"Right."

"So where did you stash the physical me?"

"Safe place. Bad man will not look there."

"Okay, but will Rafe be able to find me there? Because I'm pretty sure he'll be looking for me."

Enkou paused between a *squish* and a *thump*. "Good thinking, Sage," he said approvingly. "Be right back." *Thump*. And he disappeared.

Gingerly, I lay back down on the grass and closed my eyes. It might be the only rest I would get for some time to come.

Chapter 9

"Roman," I panted as we followed Rafe, "one more question."

"Sure."

I don't know why I thought it would be a good idea to initiate a conversation just then. I was already gulping air, and now I had to try to talk. "What's Ingun's...interest in...Ingrid?" I managed.

"You got that She hates White Buffalo Calf Pipe Woman, right?"

"Yeah," I gasped.

"Well, I think Ingun got wind of your goddess's plan to ensure another generation of Curtises as acolytes to the gods, and decided enough was enough."

"Witherspoons," I said.

"What?"

"It's Mom's line...She's...interested in."

"Oh. Well, whatever." The guy wasn't even winded. I was starting to hate him for his youth. "The point is that She perceived it as a power play. So She went out and recruited Her own Chosen."

"Heir," I said. "Mom's the...Chosen."

"Whatever."

"So Ingun's Heir is Ingrid?" I said on a long exhale that left my lungs burning, and sucked in several short breaths to try to recover.

"You got it. And She and Loki want Rex to be the father."

"Because..."

"Good looks, powerful political connections, hardly any brains." He grinned. "Thought I'd help you save your breath."

"Thanks." I grinned back. It all made sense, and if I'd had two minutes of peace to think things through, I probably would have figured it out myself. "One more."

"Yeah?"

"Who's Rex's god?" I mean, he had to have one; everybody else in the family did. I had a couple of candidates – Adonis, maybe, or Narcissus – but I wanted to see if Roman would tell me.

No luck. He merely gave me a mysterious smile and sped up to draw even with Rafe.

I shrugged mentally. It probably wouldn't make any difference. Rex was, at best, a bit player in this drama. Still, it's always a good idea to have your scorecard completely filled out.

We pushed through a fire door and into a cave — not as big as the one the gods had made for Rafe's climate-change project, but impressive in its own way. The military had hacked out a series of long channels in the gutrock and filled them with water. Just inside the entrance and up a set of metal steps was an open door. Through the doorway, I could see computer equipment, probably to manage the water levels and send it wherever in the complex it needed to go. But the far end of the control shack was filled with a blooming hazel tree. The roots had broken through the floor in several places — seeking the water in the reservoir, I assumed — and the back corner of the shack drooped at an odd angle.

"That's where Rivers was holding Sage," Rafe said, pointing at the shack.

"I'm guessing the tree isn't standard equipment," I said.

"No." He shot me a brief grin. "That's how she got away from him. When the wall began to give way, she slipped out the hole." He gazed darkly at the shack. "We were almost out of here."

"Where's Rivers?" I asked. "Did you see where he went?"

He shook his head. "Like I said, he was unconscious when I left."

"Hey, guys," Leonard called. "I found him."

We followed his voice to the far side of the control shack. There, shoved among the roots of the tree, was Jack Rivers. His hands and feet had been bound with thin roots; more roots bound some sort of gag in his mouth. He groaned and began to struggle, the whites of his eyes showing as he looked at each of us in turn.

Leonard leaned over the old man and said, in a menacing tone, "Here's the deal, Rivers. I take off the gag, and you tell what you know. If you don't cooperate, you'll get worse than a gag. Is that clear?"

Rivers made some unintelligible sounds, but eventually nodded. Leonard unwound the roots, which had tightened as they dried and left crimson weals on his face. As the last of the roots came loose, Rivers spat out the thing that had been stuffed in his mouth, and it rolled, zigzagging, away from him. I saw what it was even before it came to a stop at my feet: it was half a cucumber.

I fell to the floor beside it, helpless with laughter.

"*¡Hijo de perra! ¡Chinga tu madre!*" Rivers roared at me.

That only made me laugh harder. "*¡Ay, viejo!*" I said, when I could catch my breath. "*¡Qué divertísimo! Quiere usted que chingar mi madre, pero ¡ella no le chingará nunca!*"

"*Te mataré,*" he growled, and lunged at me, forgetting he was still tied up, which made me start laughing again.

"*¡Basta!*" yelled Rafe. "Cut it out, Webb! You're wasting time."

"Sorry," I said, wiping my eyes. "I couldn't help it. I just kept picturing Enkou stuffing that cucumber in his mouth." I giggled. "And then he told me to go screw my mother, which is hilarious because...well, you know." I swallowed a laugh and cleared my throat. "Sorry. I'm better now."

Roman had his hand to his mouth. It just about covered his smirk.

Rafe gave me his best long-suffering look, then rounded on Rivers. "Where's my wife, you son of a bitch?" he demanded.

"I don't know," Rivers said, sneering.

I heard a splash behind me, and turned to see my favorite ninja turtle pulling himself out of the nearest reservoir. "Hey, Enkou," I said. "Nice work here."

He grunted as he padded up to us. "Looking for Sage?" he asked me.

"As a matter of fact, we are."

"Come." And he headed back to the reservoir.

"Hey, wait a minute," I called, and he turned. "Where is she, underwater? You know I can't swim as well as you."

"For gods' sake, Webb!" Rafe said, and strode past me to Enkou. "Let's go."

"Good," the kappa said, and dove in. Rafe was right behind him.

I watched them disappear. If this reservoir was anything like the one we'd encountered in the gods' realm years ago, there would be a plug near the bottom – not a bathtub-type plug, probably, but a valve that led to a water main. My guess is that he'd taken my sister through the valve and into one of those pipes, or else a chamber adjacent to those pipes. More likely a chamber, in case someone began drawing down the reservoir. In any case, I had no idea how long it would take for them to get there, pick up Sage, and get back. And how would they transport her?

"Maybe I should follow them," I said.

"Why?" asked Leonard, as if it were one of the craziest things I'd ever said.

"I could make her a waterproof sack, so she could breathe while they brought her back. I mean, what if she's unconscious? She could drown before they get back here."

"Webb," Leonard said. "You're babbling."

"No, I'm not. I'm serious. Rafe didn't think this through." I got to my feet. "I'm going in."

"Too late, Galahad," Roman said, nodding toward the reservoir behind me. I spun, and beheld a blue-black raven shooting out of the water with Sage draped across his back. A knot in my chest loosened, but not by much.

Rafe began to shift as he landed; we hurried to his side and eased her off his back to the floor. She was unconscious, but breathing, and her eyelids fluttered as she began to come around.

"We need to get her out of here," Rafe said. "She needs medical attention." He pointed through the gap in her shirt to the mud that oozed away from her side.

"Don't touch," Sage said weakly. "Poultice."

A mud poultice? I hoped Enkou had put something medicinal underneath. "Who ripped your shirt?" I said.

"Jack," Sage said faintly.

Rivers, who had clearly heard us, was giggling to himself. "Such small *chichis*," he said. "Naomi's are bigger."

Rafe took a step toward the old man, who was still held fast amid the tree roots. "You son of a bitch. If you touched my wife…"

Leonard stepped in front of him. "Get a grip," he advised. "He's nothing. You hear me? *Nothing.* Focus on Sage."

Rafe glared at Rivers, who was still giggling, and stepped back to my sister. He crouched next to her head and whispered to her, "We're gonna get you out of here, honey."

"That would be nice," she said, her eyes still shut. He took her hand.

"Where's Enkou?" I asked.

Rafe looked up at me. "He said he had to finish something."

"The weir in Dad's timestream," Sage said.

"What?" I knelt next to her head on the opposite side. "What about Dad's timestream?"

"He took me there," she said, and winced. "Enkou. He said…*fuck*, it hurts." She grimaced for a moment, gripping Rafe's hand tightly. Then her expression eased a fraction. "He said he told you."

I looked up at Leonard. "He told us he needed to protect Dad from the darkness. I thought he meant Ingrid's glamor."

"So did I," Leonard said.

"But I fixed that with the amulets," I said. "What other darkness is he talking about?" I was getting pretty sick and tired of mysteries.

"Where *is* Dad?" Sage asked, her voice barely above a whisper.

Rafe and I exchanged surprised looks. "We met up with him at the trailhead," I said. "He said he was going after you. You never saw him?"

"No."

"Shit," I said. "That was hours ago. *Shit.*" This was no time for him to go walkabout.

Rivers laughed, a high-pitched, haunting sound. "Going to see Naomi," he crooned. "Going to see her *chichis.*"

"Somebody gag him again," I said.

"With pleasure," said Leonard. He scooped up the cucumber on his way.

"She needs an ambulance," Rafe said, pulling out his phone. He looked at it, scowled, and shoved it back in his pocket. "I can't get a signal in here."

"Let's get her to the car," I said. "If we still can't get a signal out there, we can drive her to a hospital."

"Hey, look what I found," Roman said, pointing to a cabinet marked **EMERGENCY SUPPLIES**. Inside it, we found gauze, over-the-counter pain medications, and the sort of emergency-carry board I'd seen at public pools, complete with a set of straps.

It was slow work getting Sage on the board. She screamed once when we moved too fast. "Jesus, she's bleeding through the mud," Rafe muttered. I saw what he was talking about: a spot on the mudpack was darkening. We emptied the supply cabinet of gauze and wrapped it all around her middle, leaving Enkou's poultice in place underneath.

Moments later, we got to our feet and carefully picked up the board. "What do we do about him?" Leonard asked, jerking his chin toward Rivers.

"Leave him," I said. "We'll come back for him once we get Sage to the hospital."

In retrospect, it was a dumb decision. But I was focused on saving my sister, and anyway, all four of us were needed to carry the board. We had no one to spare to stay behind and keep an eye on Rivers.

We found a rhythm that didn't jostle my sister too much; still, she passed out about halfway through our journey. As we made our way past the blast doors, a klaxon went off.

"They must have found Ingun," Roman shouted. "Let's move!"

Speed became more important than stability. We raced for the end of the tunnel, the klaxon nearly deafening us. But just as we thought we'd made it, a phalanx of armed men stepped into our path, blocking the exit.

"Wounded!" Roman yelled. "Clear the way! Emergency!"

"Nice try," said a familiar voice, dripping with sarcasm, and from out of the shadows stepped Loki. "Roman, Roman, Roman. Whatever gave you the idea that you could break into My compound and forcibly restrain a member of My staff?"

"I'm not Your staff," Ingun said angrily, sliding toward us from the other side of the tunnel. Then Her voice turned sultry. "Hello, boys. It's nice to see you again. We never got to finish our business last time, did we?" She brushed Her shoulder against mine as She passed me.

"I didn't mean You, My sweet," said Loki. "I meant him."

And from the shadows behind us came the hated, singsong voice of Jack Rivers. "Going to see Naomi. Going to lick her *chichis*. Going to see Naomi!" I thought he would stop and taunt us further, but instead he ran right past us to the tunnel entrance.

"Oh, that's right," Loki said, clapping his hands once. "How could I forget? We have a surprise outside for you. Come along!" And He prodded Roman into motion with the toe of His boot.

"I'm coming, I'm coming," Roman muttered, as we started moving again.

"My wife needs medical attention," Rafe said hotly.

"All in good time, My dear Raven," Loki said, sounding smug. "All in good time."

As we stepped out of the tunnel into the frigid parking lot, I heard someone call my name. "Oh, no," I said faintly.

"Oh, yes," said Loki with glee.

Sure enough, standing in the parking lot, surrounded by Neo-Atheists bristling with guns, were my girlfriend Hilary and my mother.

Chapter 10

It was a lousy moment to suddenly find myself hovering within the Universal web.

To be clear, this wasn't my timestream simulation, or even that other, bigger simulation of the web: this was the web itself. Not to get too technical – or too airy-fairy, depending on how you feel about it – but there are ways you can tell it's the real thing. Simulations always have a sense of remove about them, no matter how good they are; you always know, in the back of your mind, that it's only for practice. The real web doesn't have any failsafes – no escape hatches, no do-overs, and no way to reboot. Unless you count something like Ragnarok.

So my presence here had all the earmarks of divine meddling. Somebody – capital-S Somebody – wanted me to yank on one of these strands. But I didn't know who, or why, or which strand I was supposed to touch. Nevertheless, apparently I wasn't going to be sent back until it was done.

I calmed my breathing and considered the situation. The bad guys were all accounted for, as far as I knew: Loki and Ingun were both at Cheyenne Mountain. With my family.

I calmed my breathing again. Even as ill as Mom was, she was not without resources; she was still capable of *pushing* the gods into doing what she wanted them to do. And Hilary had Enkou, who had lately developed a knack for being in the right place at the right time.

Not to mention Rafe, who was a trained fighter, with Raven's intelligence and cunning. Leonard, too, had a few tricks up his sleeve. And Roman had turned into a formidable ally.

No, my role there was ancillary. My secret weapon was right here, around me. If only I could figure out which strand...

I found my own easily enough, although as usual I couldn't learn anything useful from it – other than that Hilary's strand entwined with mine for a good, long while to come. My stomach settled a little bit. Things could still change, of course, depending on what I did here, as well as millions of other factors I couldn't see. Not for the first time, I cursed the psychic myopia that kept me from seeing anything I had a hand in.

I resisted the urge to touch Hilary's strand, and moved on.

I found Mom's strand, too, and the darkness hovering around it. Her future was clouded – which didn't mean she was going to die for sure, I sternly told myself. Rather, it meant we were reaching a decision point: either Ingun would agree to stop messing with Mom, or She wouldn't. I wondered if I were supposed to reach in there – just a little tweak, to break Ingun's hold on my mother and allow her to heal. But Aunt Shannon had tried that multiple times, and Ingun had always managed to get back in. I needed something as powerful as Ingun, either to restrain Her or to slip into the breach and protect Mom from any further assaults, or both.

I went hunting for White Buffalo Calf Pipe Woman's strand, and found it – in its usual spot, hovering near Mom's. I saw the tangle where they'd fought, and the wide divergence since then. But there was an odd bobble in the tangle, as if the goddess had removed something deliberately. And that act seemed tangential to the disagreement. In fact, it looked as if She had staged the argument as a cover-up.

Frowning, I followed that bit of broken strand forward, and my suspicion was confirmed. That lack was how Ingun had gotten in.

This is why I preferred my timestream model; I could have immersed myself in the moment and seen exactly what the goddess had removed. Here, I had to guess. But it seemed logical that in that moment, White Buffalo Calf Pipe Woman had stopped protecting my mother's health.

That explained why Mom had suddenly begun to look so old, and why her cancer had taken root so easily. But it begged another question: Had the goddess deliberately cleared the way for Ingun?

I couldn't believe that. I'd seen Her angry reaction to the news that Ingun was harming my mother. White Buffalo Calf Pipe Woman was a lot of things, but She was no actress. And too, She had said to me, *You may find it hard to believe, with all that has happened, but I love you all.*

She might have been blowing smoke when She said that, but I didn't think so.

So why *had* the goddess pulled Her health boost from Mom? And why hadn't She put it back yet? Their strands were so close.

She was waiting for something. Or someone. Me?

Just a nudge would do it...

My fingers reached for the strands, but I snatched them back. I needed more information.

I circled around the muddy mess that was the present moment I'd been pulled out of, and inventoried the strands leading into it: Sage and Rafe, check; Leonard, Roman, and me, check; Mom and Hilary, check; Loki and Ingun, check; and Jack Rivers, check. There were probably a dozen others – the Neo-Atheists surrounding Mom and Hilary, and reinforcements nearby, I supposed. And heading there fast was another contingent, protecting someone in the middle. I wove my way through the cordon and found two strands inside: those belonging to President Holt and the former First Lady.

I sidled up to Antonia Greco's strand, as close as I could get without touching it, and whispered, "Tell Darrell." The strand vibrated slightly from my breath, but nothing around it changed; I had to assume that meant JAF-H/D had already been informed.

I turned to leave, but then thought of something else. Leaning in again, I whispered, "Roman is amazing." Again, her strand moved a tiny bit – and brightened perceptibly. Satisfied, I scooted out through a gap and hovered near the muddy mess again.

That accounted for everyone except my father. I looked around again, and spotted him at last, high above the fray and dropping fast. I moved up to meet him, and...

...my perceptions shifted, and I felt as if I were in four places at once. My consciousness was still inside the Universal web, but I could feel my physical self crumpled in a heap next to Sage's makeshift stretcher, Leonard kneeling next to me. And I saw the scene from two angles: ground level across the parking lot, and high above, riding an air current.

A fierce sense of freedom rose within me. *This is so cool! How can Sage not love flying?*

Two startled voices replied: *Webb?*

Mom? How did you get in here?

Never mind that, said Dad. *How did* you *get in here?*

I dunno. I was in the Universal web and I saw your strand, and all of a sudden…

What are you doing in the web? Mom demanded. *Hilary is frantic.* She turned so I could see my girlfriend's face streaked with tears.

I ached to comfort her. *For gods' sake, Mom! Tell her I'm okay.*

I couldn't hear the real-life conversation, but I saw Mom take her hand and whisper to her. Hilary's eyes widened and she mouthed, *What? How?* Then she nodded and wiped her eyes with the back of her hand.

Thanks, I told Mom. *For the record, leaving wasn't my idea.*

Whose idea was it? Dad said.

I wish I knew. Can we get closer? I can't hear what's going on.

Oh, Dad said, and at once I could hear everything – the wind whistling past my father's avian ears, the guards shifting behind my mother, and Loki's gleeful speech. Unfortunately, I heard Loki in stereo: first through Mom's ears, and then echoed a moment later through Dad's.

"Your concern for your fallen comrade is touching," Loki was saying, "but misplaced. Look at how he has abandoned you in your hour of need." He looked straight at Mom. "Naomi," He chided her. "I would have thought you'd have trained your children better."

"Let's talk about how *your* children turned out," Mom said.

That wiped the smile from His face. *Nice one, Mom,* I said.

Shh, said Dad.

"Look," Mom went on. "This has gone on long enough. Give me my children and I promise we won't trouble You any further."

"Oh, yes, you will," said Ingun. "You'll figure out a way to get around your promise, and you'll still come to Our realm to fix that awful agreement. I'm not going to lose to your precious goddess again!" Then She gave her a cruel smile. "But then again, you won't be alive long enough to negotiate anything, will you?"

"Yes, yes, it's all very sad. Enough of that," said Loki, grinning fiendishly again. "We have a surprise for you, Naomi. It's someone I'm certain you'll be glad to see again." He gestured theatrically, and Jack Rivers stepped out from a puff of oily smoke, right next to Sage's prone form.

Oh, no, I thought.

"Gods, no," Mom breathed.

Fuck, my father said. His field of vision – which was mine as well – narrowed to a slit in a sea of black.

Enkou had said the weir he was building in my father's timestream was for protection against *the darkness*. All at once, I figured out which darkness he'd meant. Moreover, I figured out what he'd been up to. Enkou hadn't meant to stop the darkness; he'd meant to channel it, so it would be released at the proper time. Which was going to be pretty soon.

Hold it together, Dad, I said. *Not yet.*

Meanwhile, Jack had dropped to his knees. "Such little *chichis*," he sang, reaching for my sister.

Rafe, his face dark with anger, lunged – and froze. Loki laughed at him. "Oh, no, you don't," He said. "Jack just wants to play. Don't you, Jack?"

"Little *chichis*," he sang, squeezing my sister's breasts. "Naomi's are bigger. Want to see Naomi." He turned to Loki. "Get to see Naomi! You promised!"

"She's here," Loki said, and gestured toward my mother.

He squinted in her direction. Mom stepped forward.

NO! Dad yelled.

But Mom wouldn't listen. "I'm right here, Jack," she said, raising her arms toward him. "You can have me. But not until Loki lets my children go."

NO! Dad yelled again. A *skree* of anguish tore from his avian throat, and he began to descend.

Not yet! I cried. *Hold on!*

Can't! I should have killed that fucker when I had the chance!

Jack, meanwhile, had left my sister and stepped uncertainly toward Mom. "Naomi?" he said, still squinting.

"Yes, Jack. It's really me. I've left Joseph for you at last. After Loki lets Sage and Webb go, you can do whatever you want to me." Her words were brave, but I could feel her disgust and desperation. Her sacrifice was both endearing and horrifying.

"Whatever…?" His face lit briefly. Then he scowled. "Not Naomi."

"What do you mean, Jack?" she said, confused. "Of course it's me."

"Not Naomi," he insisted. "Too old to be Naomi." He buried his face in his hands and began to sob.

Mom, to her credit, gathered him into her arms.

She doesn't mean it! I cried, as Dad let loose with another *skree*. He was losing altitude rapidly; in another few seconds, he'd be right on top of Mom and Jack.

Except Jack had thrown off my mother's embrace, knocking her backward onto the pavement. She looked up at him, dazed. "Not Naomi!" he screamed, and raised his hand to strike her. Then he screamed again as twin red lasers burned holes in his back. Sage had managed to get her head up high enough to shoot.

Dad, be careful! I yelled.

I don't know whether he understood me, but clearly he realized Jack was no longer a threat. He changed course to avoid my sister's laser fire, and headed instead for the source of all the trouble: Loki.

Jack was still screaming. Then laser fire shot out from his chest; Sage's eyes had burned straight through him. He collapsed on top of Mom's legs.

In a flash of argent light, White Buffalo Calf Pipe Woman materialized next to Hilary. "Now, Webb!" She cried.

Inside the Universal web, I nudged my mother's strand. It snapped away from Ingun's, and White Buffalo Calf Pipe Woman's rushed in to close the gap.

Back in the parking lot, Ingun screamed. "You arrogant bitch!" I heard Her cry at Mom's goddess.

But I couldn't see what happened next, because Mom's consciousness blinked out, and Dad was focused on Loki's horrified face as we made for Him, talons out.

And then I was back in my own body. I sat up and shook my head to clear it. Sage was out again, her surge of adrenaline spent. Loki was yelling as he tried to pry a golden eagle off of His face. And a contingent of large black SUVs converged on the parking lot from multiple directions. "Secret Service!" shouted the first man out of a vehicle. "Hands up! Drop your weapons!"

The Neo-Atheists, confronted with trained agents who actually knew what to do with guns, obeyed.

With Loki's attention elsewhere, Rafe and Leonard had regained their power of movement. Rafe was next to Sage, watching her anxiously, while Leonard jogged toward the nearest agent to ask for an ambulance. I gripped Rafe's shoulder. Then I got to my feet and made my unsteady way toward my girlfriend, who met me halfway.

"Good morning," she said, once the preliminaries were over.

My eyebrows shot up, and I glanced toward the horizon. Sure enough, the sky there was pink and orange, and brightening as we watched. "Good morning," I returned. "I could sleep for a week. Roman ran me ragged."

Over Hilary's head, I saw Antonia Greco jump from one of the vehicles and run to my mother. "Naomi, are you all right?"

Mom sat up and shook her head, much as I had just done. "I'm fine," she said in wonder.

"What's happened to you?" Antonia said, sitting back on her heels. "You look so much younger."

The goddess glided over to my mother and offered her a hand up, then wrapped her in an embrace. "I am sorry," She said. "Taking your health protection was the only way I could think to save you." She threw a venomous glance at Ingun, who approached them with fire in Her eye. "I had no idea *that* one would take advantage of it."

"And why wouldn't I?" Ingun said. "You – You New World upstart! You'll never be fit for a seat in Valhalla! *I* should be in charge!"

"You?" The goddess's laugh was rich with scorn. "So You can make a disaster of Our realm the same way You've done here on Earth? Ingun, listen to Me. Loki is *using You*. He has no interest in ruling over either Our realm or Earth. He only wants power so He can cause trouble."

"White Buffalo Calf Pipe Woman speaks the truth," said Freya, joining the group. "It has ever been thus with Loki, as well You know."

"What do You know of anything?" Ingun sneered. "You're another upstart! And You stole My followers! You know nothing of the elder days, and you know nothing of love. Nothing!"

Freya shone with a golden light. "I know that I love *You*, Ingun, for You are part of Me." She took the shocked elder goddess into Her arms. "Come. Let's go home. Frey is asking after You."

Diana appeared next to Antonia. "You know She wanted you dead," She told Naomi.

Mom nodded. "I'd gathered that. Thanks for Your timely arrival. Even though You brought *him* with You." Her lip curled as she gestured toward former President Holt, who was trying to convince Dad the Eagle to stop pecking at Loki's face. "Joseph!" she called. "It's over. Let Him go."

It was indeed over. The ambulance arrived for Sage as three Black Ops helicopters set down inside the Secret Service perimeter. Diana and Morrigan, the Irish goddess of war, grabbed Loki to haul Him away. Dad grabbed my backpack in his talons and flew into the tunnel; mere moments later, he emerged, fully dressed.

Roman ambled up. "How does he *do* that so fast?" he asked.

"I told you. Years of practice."

"Son," the President said, brushing past Roman on his way to intercept my father. I saw the shadow that crossed Roman's expression, and squeezed his shoulder wordlessly.

"Ah," he said with a shrug. "It's okay. I'm used to it."

The President planted himself between my parents. "Joseph," he said, scowling. "Have you no self-control?"

Mom snorted. "You're a fine one to talk about self-control, Brock. Don't think I don't know who shredded my files after we broke up."

The President eyed her over his shoulder. "Way to hold a grudge, Naomi. How many decades have you been holding onto that?"

"Are we still alive?" she shot back. "Then not nearly long enough."

At the hospital...

I remembered very little of what happened after I got shot. I'm told I came to a couple of times, and even gave the guys some useful information at one point.

I do remember coming awake when Rivers manhandled my boobs. Mainly I lasered him because his pathetic whining about Mom not being Mom was keeping me from going back to sleep. Plus, you know, I hated him by then. So now Dad and I have another thing in common besides flying.

Anyway, after that, everything was mixed up. I think I remember a little bit of the ambulance ride, but I was pretty dizzy – whether from blood loss or from the drugs they were pumping into me, I'm not sure. I do remember Rafe being there with me.

He was with me at the hospital, too, when I woke up.

I tried to sit up and groaned. My side was pretty sore. "How long have I been out?"

He kissed my forehead and took my hand – the one that didn't have the IV in it. "Maybe twelve hours. Thanksgiving is tomorrow."

"I guess I won't be eating turkey at Mom and Dad's," I said with a sigh.

"They're holding off dinner for you," he said with a smile. "As long as it takes."

I smiled back for a moment. Then I asked, "How bad was it?"

"Not bad," he said, although his expression said, *not exactly a walk in the park, either.* "The bullet grazed the lowest rib on that side and stopped. It was lucky you were shifted when you were hit, though. You cauterized your own wound."

I gave him a half-smile. "Thunderbird is finally good for something."

"Thunderbird is good for a *lot*," he said. He stared at our joined hands for a moment, then looked up at me. "I was really worried. I kept thinking about how much I didn't want to lose you."

I smiled and kissed his hand. "What happened after I fell in the reservoir? I think I had a conversation with Enkou, as weird as that sounds."

"Not weird at all. He saved you from drowning in the reservoir and stashed you in a maintenance tunnel. He even made a poultice for your wound."

"I remember the poultice!" I said, trying to push up again.

"Here," Rafe said. He eased me forward and braced me on his shoulder while he fixed my pillows.

I nestled my cheek against his collarbone. "I could just stay here," I sighed.

He chuckled and gave me a gentle hug before re-situating me. "Better?"

"Yeah."

"So yeah, the poultice." He sat back down in the chair. "The doc said it probably saved your life. Kept the wound from getting infected and kept the bullet from working its way in any deeper."

"Go, Enkou," I said. "So then what happened?"

And he told me about how he dodged Rivers' gunfire, disarmed him, and knocked him out, then dove in to try to find me. "I was frantic at that point," he said. "I knew I had to find you, but I needed help. So I went to get the other guys." And then he told me about how they found Rivers tied up with a cucumber stuffed in his mouth, which made me laugh – which made my side hurt like hell, but I kind of didn't care. And then he told me about how Enkou led him to me, and how he did everything he could to get me to safety. He wasn't blowing his own horn – not at all. And that, as much as what he said, told me how much he loved me.

"I'm glad you didn't give up," I said when he wound down. "I'm glad I'm still here to tell you I love you."

Then he held me for real. I wanted to tell him more, but just that little bit of conversation had worn me out and I fell asleep in his arms.

The next time I awoke, I felt tons better. My side still twinged when I shifted position – I supposed it would for a while – but my head was clearer, and I remembered there was something I still needed to do.

Rafe was at my bedside, dozing in the chair and looking adorable. "Hi," I said.

He came upright in a hurry. "Hi."

I giggled. "Sorry. You can go back to sleep if you want."

"No, I'm fine." He yawned and stretched. "What can I get for you? Anything?"

"A kiss, for starters." I made sure it lasted a long time. And then I said, "Where are my jeans?"

"You can't go home yet," he said. "Doctor's orders. And Darrell said to take the rest of the week off."

"How very kind of him," I said dryly. "I already had the rest of the week off. Anyway, I'm not trying to bust out of here. I need something from the front pocket."

Dubiously, Rafe went to the little closet and pulled out my jeans, then fished around in the pockets. "Is this it?" he asked, holding it out so I could see.

"Yup, that's it." It was the nut cluster Cerridwen had given me. The leafy reddish cups the nuts had been nestled in had shriveled, and one of the remaining two nuts fell out into Rafe's palm as he extended the cluster to me. "You keep that one," I said as I took the cluster. The third one rolled out into my own hand. *One for your husband and one for you.* I smiled at the memory.

He rolled the nut around with his fingers. "Looks like a hazelnut," he said.

"Yeah?"

"Yeah. Where'd you get them from?"

"Cerridwen gave them to me. I planted the first one at the reservoir."

He'd glanced up at me at the mention of my goddess. "Did She say what we were supposed to do with them?" he asked. "Plant them?"

"No, only one was to plant. I think we're supposed to eat them."

He shrugged. "Far be it from me to countermand a direct order from a goddess." He put his nut on the bedside table, picked up the water glass, and brought it down hard on the nut. The shell split into impossibly even halves. He tossed the shells in the trash and set the perfect nutmeat aside. "Want me to do the honors?" he asked, holding out his hand for my nut.

"I think I'd better do it," I said, and picked up the water glass. My nutmeat was almost more perfect than his.

"Are we supposed to say a few words?" he said, a smile playing around his mouth.

I shrugged and smiled. "No clue."

"'Over the teeth and past the gums,'" he said.

"'Look out, stomach, here it comes,'" I finished, and popped the nut in my mouth.

It tasted like a hazelnut. But then something in my chest began to feel loose – unaccountably so – as if a locked door had opened and joy poured through it. It spread throughout my body, cleansing me of all the ugly emotional residue that had ever lodged itself in my tissues: anger at the goddess over my powers, fear and self-loathing from the rape, disgust from Rivers' mauling, and – surprisingly – guilt I hadn't realized I was carrying for ending the lives of the men who had attacked me. It even pre-emptively took out any regret I would feel at killing Jack Rivers. All of the emotions that were blocking me from reconciling with Rafe were burned away, leaving nothing but peace in their wake.

I looked at Rafe with new eyes, and saw him looking at me the same way.

It was another couple of days before the doctor pronounced me recovered enough to go home. But in my heart, I knew I was already well.

Chapter 11

I thought Mom might let me off the hook for the mediation session, seeing as how her cancer was finally in remission and she was feeling stronger by the day. But no dice.

"If anything," she told me one morning, "I'm more determined now to make sure one of you is trained in my techniques. I've had a serious brush with mortality, Webb. I need to see to my legacy." She brought toast and coffee to the kitchen table, and sat down to join me for breakfast. "And even the god-kissed die eventually. If not, Looks Far would still be with us."

"I get that," I said. "But Sage had a brush with mortality, too. Maybe she'll come around now to the idea of taking on the family business."

Mom shook her head. "Your sister has a profession."

"So do I!" I protested.

"Noted," she said. "Let me put it another way: Your sister has a job that brings her a steady paycheck. Job security. So does Rafe."

"So does Hilary," I said, but I knew my position was weak.

"But you don't," she finished. "Mediation work isn't a steady paycheck unless you sign on with a firm. But it's more stable than making yourself crazy every few months over a grant you may or may not get."

"I know."

"And you can *do* this, Webb," she said, leaning in. "I've seen you speak truth to power all your life. And your suggestions always turn out to be the best course of action for all involved, whether you know the parties well or not."

Yeah, well, that part's easy if you can drop into their timestreams and see the future. I sighed. "All right."

"Good," she said. "That's settled. Did you bring the books I gave you? We have a few hours this morning to prepare."

"Yeah. I'll go get them." I'd packed them with the hope I could just give them back to her. But it looked like I was in for it now.

We had more time than that to prepare, as it turned out. Mom had forgotten that she couldn't just tell the gods to show up at a certain time tomorrow, and They'd do it. The gods had schedules, it turned out – schedules They had to clear in order to meet with us.

Plus the entrances to the gods' realm, while no longer patrolled by Loki, were still as difficult to get through as they ever were. The gods themselves could come and go again, but humans risked life, limb, and sanity to get there without divine intervention.

"We don't even know the issues, really," Mom said to me on Saturday morning, as we waited for Rafe to bring Sage home. Hilary and Grandma were in the kitchen, working on the last-minute dishes for our delayed Thanksgiving feast. Dad had gone in to work, and Leonard had gone hiking in the national forest that abutted our property. "We need to have a pre-meeting with one or more of the gods to find out what's been going on up there."

"Ragnarok," I said.

"I know that," she said, "but why? Loki can't have started it all by Himself. We know Ingun went along with it because She wanted power…"

"She wanted to be remembered," I said. "That's why She went along with Loki. She believed Freya stole all Her followers and She wanted them back. But Freya is a later manifestation of Ingun. She didn't steal Her followers; She subsumed Ingun's essence into Herself. Ingun sees that as a betrayal," I went on. "She sees Herself the same way a jilted lover would. But it's not what happened. What Ingun really needs is to be independent again."

Mom was sitting back in her chair, tapping her fingertips together and watching me.

"What?" I said.

She sat forward and dropped her hands to the arms of her chair. "So, Counselor," she said, "outline for me what you believe are the major issues we need to settle."

"Well," I said, easing back into approximately the same posture my mother had just abandoned, "we need to identify who the disgruntled parties are, and work Them into the fabric of the agreement. Give Them a voice, or a job all Their own. Maybe it will be enough to simply hear Their grievances and send Them on Their way – kind of like you used to do with Sage and me." I put my hands together and pointed at her with both forefingers.

"Go on."

"We need to make sure Loki is neutralized to the point where He can't make this much trouble again," I said.

"It's up to the gods to discipline Him, though. Isn't it?"

"Is it? It's our realm He was causing trouble in. Can't we at least ask Them to keep a better eye on Him?"

Mom looked away. "We can ask. But They will put it back on me. I'm the one who persuaded Odin to release Him from His original punishment."

"So do a *mea culpa.*"

Her eyes widened. "Naomi Witherspoon, admit to the gods that she made a mistake? You're expecting a lot from me, Counselor."

"Say you've had a recent brush with mortality," I said. "So you're anxious to make things right."

"Now you're throwing my words back at me."

"How good of you to notice." We shared a grin. Then I said, "You know, there's another big question we need Them to answer."

"Whether They're staying or leaving," Mom said with a sigh. "Yes, I know. And I don't know how to ask without bringing your sister into it."

"What about Ingrid?" I asked.

"What about her?"

I chose my words carefully. "I wonder whether she's still interested in Rex," I said. "And if she is, whether there's more to it than meets the eye."

"You've never liked her," Mom said. "She seems like a perfectly nice…"

"Mom," I said. "She. Tried. To. Eat. Me."

"What?" she said, laughing in disbelief.

"It was months ago. I'm sure I told you. I had a dream that an Icelandic princess unhinged her jaws and tried to swallow me head-first."

"I vaguely recall this," she said after a moment. "Was this at the same time when Lucifer was showing up in your dreams?"

I nodded emphatically. "And as soon as I saw Ingrid at that state reception at the Holts', I knew she was the woman in my dream." I squinted at her. "Are you still wearing the amulet I made for you?"

Her fingers flew to her throat. "I think so. I don't remember taking it off."

I got up from my chair and put my fingers just below the notch at the base of her throat. There was a warm, springy spot that didn't correlate to any anatomical drawing I'd ever seen. "It's still there. Sorry for being fresh." I gave her a cockeyed grin as I sat back down.

"It's not like you haven't seen it all before," Mom said, straightening her collar. "I breastfed you, after all."

"That was thirty-five years ago!" Then I saw the twinkle in her eye, and lowered my eyebrows. "Way to embarrass your grown son, Mom. That was worthy of a Trickster."

She wiggled her eyebrows. "I guess living with your father is rubbing off on me."

It's not that I didn't think I could conduct mediations. As my mother said, I had a knack for it, and not just because I know the future. The question was whether I wanted to spend the time to get certified and build a practice – time I could be spending on my art. As frustrating and financially unstable as the fiber arts were, I knew I couldn't give them up. It would have been like losing a part of myself. Not that I'd equate setting aside my art to losing a limb, say. But I was a much happier camper if I could spend a significant part of most days working in my studio.

But this wasn't a conversation I could have with either of my parents. Out of everyone in our extended family – with all of our various mundane and divinely-granted talents and proclivities – I was the only artist. Ask any one of them to give up their magical talent and they'd balk. But ask them to equate that with my art, and I'd get a deer-in-the-headlights look. And yes, I know this from experience.

Anyway, I told myself this mediation session in the gods' realm was going to be a one-and-done. Mom needed backup on this specific project, and I was in a position to help her out, so I was helping her out. That's what you do for family. But if she thought I was going to continue to help her out in the future – or if she intended to train me to take over her practice – she needed to understand that there was no guarantee, and the answer was probably going to be no.

And I fully intended to tell her all that, once this project was over.

Hilary agreed with my take on it. After all, she was the one who got to live with the cranky badger I became if I wasn't working on an art project. And she wasn't overly sold on my mother's plan for me to take over her practice. In fact, she didn't even want me doing *this* mediation.

We talked about it the night after our belated Thanksgiving celebration. It was great to see everyone around the table, and all looking pretty well, for the most part, although Mom looked like the picture of health next to my sister. Sage was still pale and ate like a bird – not a Thunderbird, a real one – and went to bed very early, with Rafe right behind her. They seemed to have patched things up, although it was anyone's guess whether it would stick.

I didn't have to guess, of course. I'd peeked at her timestream, now that my part in her drama was over.

No, I'm not going to tell you what I saw.

Anyway, our recent adventures with the gods had left everyone in the family a little skittish, including my girlfriend. "I don't want you going anywhere near the gods' realm again," she said as we settled into bed. The party would be over in the morning: Leonard and Grandma were hitting the road very early, and Sage and Rafe were headed back to Washington on the hypersonic shuttle around noon. I wasn't sure how soon Hilary and I would get out the door – Mom wanted one more face-to-face session with me in the morning – but I was committed to this being our last night in my old room for at least several weeks.

I flipped off the light and settled one arm around Hilary with her head pillowed on my chest. "I'm not crazy about going up there again, either, Hotaru. But Mom's in a bind, and I said I'd help her."

"Well, she can't keep doing this. What are we going to do after the baby comes? You can't be at her beck and call all the time. *Our* family will have to be your first priority."

"Hey," I said, lifting her chin so my eyes could meet hers. "What's this about?"

She burst into tears. In between her sobs, she told me again how scared she had been when I'd collapsed in the parking lot outside Cheyenne Mountain.

"But Hotaru, I was fine."

"But I didn't know that!" She reached across me for a tissue from the box on the bedside table. "You just dropped. Sage was already hurt, and you looked awful, and then you just…" She blew her nose. "And I couldn't get to you."

"Ah," I said.

"And I had no idea what had gone on in the gods' realm," she went on. "Ragnarok sounds like war."

"It *is* war." I remembered the battlefields we'd seen, and pulled her closer.

"And I don't know how the gods fight each other or anything. You could have been *killed* up there, Webb, and I had no way to help you."

I remembered, suddenly, the time I'd captured Lucifer in my old timestream simulation. It was the first time she'd ever wanted to sit with the physical me while I went on a psychic excursion. "You couldn't have helped, even if you'd been there. And then *you* would have been in harm's way, too."

"But we'd be together," she said. "And at least I'd know."

My girlfriend, the math nerd, wanted as much information about the situation as possible, so she would know exactly how worried to be.

"Tell you what," I said. "I'll tell Mom I won't do the mediation with her unless you can come along."

"Really?" She pushed herself up one elbow, eyes wide. "I wouldn't be in the way, would I? You think she'll say yes?"

"She needs me there," I said. "Of course she'll say yes."

"Absolutely not," Mom said.

I was stunned. I really had expected her to go along with the idea. "Why?"

"Well, for one thing, she's pregnant."

"What has that got to do with anything? You practically gave birth while Jehovah was signing on the dotted line!"

"Nobody signed anything," Mom said testily. "That's a common misconception."

"It was a figure of speech, Mom," I said, trying not to roll my eyes like a teenager. "Seriously, why can't she come? You and Dad had half the *world* at the last one!"

"All those people had good reasons to be there," said Mom. "They all had a part in the process."

"Hilary has, too," I said. "She helped Darrell nail the head of the Neo-Atheists, remember?"

I could see her working on a retort. When that failed, she resorted to that old parental favorite: Because I Said So. "No. Absolutely not."

I took a moment to calm myself. Then I said, "Come on. What's really bugging you?"

"She's carrying my grandchild!" she said.

"Ah."

"And you'll be busy, Webb. There won't be anyone available to keep an eye on her."

"Now you're making her sound like a four-year-old."

"That's not what I mean." She fixed me with a stern look. "Webb, think. You know there have been discussions about an Heir."

"So?"

"So you come from the same genetic material as your sister," she said, annoyed that she had to spell it out. "And to be blunt, my son, *you* have reproduced."

My stomach dropped about a foot. "Oh. Oh, no. *Hell* no."

Mom nodded sagely. "Oh, yes. So we need to keep her as far from any of the gods as possible."

"Which is *im*possible," I said, "and you know it. If one of Them wants to get to Hilary, They can find her anywhere. In fact," I said, "the mediation might be the safest place for her. If Someone tries something, we'll be right there to put a stop to it."

"Webb, no," Mom said again. "She doesn't belong there."

"Because she doesn't have a role," I said. "Here's her role, Mom: her role is that I don't go unless she does." I got up and stalked out. "We're heading home. I'll call you later."

"Webb!" she cried, but I wasn't about to turn back. If any of the gods had drawn a bead on Hotaru, I was going to make damned sure They had to go through me first.

Mom Skyped the next day to tell me she'd heard back from the goddess. I was puttering around in my studio while Hillary was at work.

Since Ragnarok had effectively annihilated Everyone's calendars, the goddess didn't need as much lead time to schedule the mediation session as She would have otherwise. "So we're all set for Wednesday," Mom told me

Wednesday was November twenty-ninth by our Earthly calendar – the day before first-round rejections were due to be announced for the big grant I'd applied for. "I guess it'll help me keep my mind off of my chances of losing," I said.

She ignored me. "The goddess wants to meet with us to go over the agenda. I'd like to take the opportunity to get the players straight in our heads, too. Sound good?"

I sighed. "Sure. When?"

In response, both Mom and the goddess materialized right there, in my studio.

"Give a guy a little warning next time, would you?" I groused. "You're lucky I'm wearing pants."

"It's not like you don't have anything I haven't seen…" Mom said.

"*Mom*," I said, glaring.

"Well, it's true." She was stifling a laugh, I could tell. I hadn't seen her this merry in months. I supposed that was a good thing, but I wasn't feeling very grateful just then.

"Come on," I said. "We'll be more comfortable in the living room." I got them settled and then started the coffeemaker. I didn't know how coffee fit into Mom's current health regimen, but I was pretty sure I would need some before this meeting was over.

"Okay," I said as I took a seat on the sofa. Mom sat primly in a chair, and the goddess had dropped into a seated cross-legged posture that would have looked perfectly natural if She hadn't been hovering a foot and a half above the ground. "First things first. We've had almost no contact with any of You for months. What's the situation there? Did Loki stage a coup, or what? And are there any other factions we need to bring to the table?"

"There have always been gods unhappy with the terms of the previous agreement," the goddess said carefully.

"That was always going to be unavoidable," said Mom, "given the size of the group. You're never going to get one hundred percent agreement with the terms of any mediated settlement; each side has to give something in order to get to a middle ground that everyone can live with. For that matter, we've had groups here on Earth that have wanted changes to the agreement."

"We've had groups that wanted to scrap the whole thing and send the gods back where They came from," I said. "Which brings me to another question. What's this about the gods maybe leaving humans to our own devices?"

"It is true," She said, "that some of Us have other interests than policing Our followers. It was a pleasant pastime for Everyone for a while, but now Some see the duties as onerous."

"They'd like to go back to contemplating Their navels," Mom said.

"We don't have navels," the goddess said with a smile. "At least, most of Us don't. Still, you have captured the essence of the argument in favor of severing ties with Earth again."

"And You, for one, would like to see a human designated as…what? A benevolent dictator to act in Your stead?" I shook my head. "Human history is rife with people who believed themselves qualified for that sort of job. It always seems to burn the benevolence right out of them, if they had any to start with, and they end up as plain old dictators. And people suffer for it."

"I am aware of that," She said. "That is why I wanted to designate a child to whom I could grant the proper abilities."

I cut a glance at my mother. "You know how lucky You got with Mom, don't You? You could have just as easily picked a kid who refused to cooperate at all."

"Like Sage," Mom said under her breath.

"Hey now," I said. "She stepped up to the plate when it mattered. She just wanted to do it on her own terms. No one can fault her for that." I turned back to the goddess. "Where do Ingrid and Rex fit into all of this?"

"You would have to ask Ingun," the goddess said. "I have not spoken to Her." She said it as if it were a virtue.

"We need to have Her at the mediation," I said. "Ingun and Loki, both. And Ingrid, too." I still wanted to know why she'd tried to eat me in my dream. Was I that much of a threat?

The goddess looked uncomfortable. "I will have to see about that. Odin has already sent Them to begin Their punishment."

"He can let Them out for a day or two," said Mom. "Webb's right. They have been the most vocal opponents to the current agreement. They need to be at this meeting." She leaned toward the goddess. "I'd be happy to talk to Odin."

"Maybe that would be best," She said. "I will arrange it."

"Mom," I said, "shouldn't we also be meeting with Loki ahead of the mediation?"

"I think He and Ingun did a pretty good job of stating Their positions at Cheyenne Mountain last week," she said.

"Okay," I said dubiously. "You're the experienced mediator here. I'm just the trainee."

Mom gave me a *don't get smart with me* look. "Ordinarily," she said with a touch of asperity, "I would agree. But not this time."

I put one hand out toward her, palm up. "Sorry. Didn't mean to cast aspersions on your decision."

Mom gave me her *you're going to catch it later* look as she turned to the goddess. "Anyone else we need to talk with before Wednesday? Jehovah?"

White Buffalo Calf Pipe Woman shook Her head. "Of all the gods, He's been the least troublesome. I think He's grateful for the help, after running Earth for so long on His own."

"Still, He should be there," said Mom.

I thought of something else. "We should have someone from the Neo-Atheists there, too. A human. There must be someone who stepped into the power vacuum when Ward Proffitt died."

Mom nodded. "Good thinking. Darrell would know who to contact."

"I'll ask Rafe." I made a note on my tablet, and then looked at the goddess. "So what's the situation in Your world? The last time we were in the usual meeting place, it was hip-deep in snow."

She sighed. "Our realm has suffered much from this war of Loki's. But I will see to it that the usual meeting place is in usable condition by Wednesday."

I swallowed hard. "What about the dead? And the Giants? Are they still roaming Your realm?"

She heaved another sigh and nodded. "I will make sure they are there, too."

"And everyone in our family should plan to be there," I said to Mom. "You and me, of course, but Dad and Sage and Rafe, as well. And Hilary," I added firmly.

"Webb, we've discussed this."

"No, we haven't. I made a request, you flat-out rejected it, and I gave you a counter-offer. I'm still waiting to hear your response."

"Andrew Joseph Curtis, you will be there on Wednesday even if I have to *push* you," Mom said, brows lowered.

I grinned. "So Hilary's invited. That's great to hear. Thanks, Mom."

The goddess was radiant with delight as she listened to this exchange. "Your mother has chosen well," She told me.

"Don't get used to it," I said. "I'm only doing this to help her out of a jam."

Mom and the goddess exchanged a glance that I definitely didn't like the look of.

Chapter 12

On the day of the mediation, Hilary and I arrived first – courtesy of Benzaiten, the Shinto goddess of all that flows, who was my girlfriend's protector. She dropped us on the vacant plain, which was now clear of snow, although the distant mountains still sported white on their peaks. I was heartened to note a few stars had returned to the skies.

"You will do fine, Webb," Benzaiten said.

"Would You please give him a blessing?" Hilary asked. "He's going to need to do a lot of persuading today, and he doesn't have his mother's gift for *pushing* people."

The goddess addressed her, but gave me a kind smile. "Ah, Hotaru, his own talents are persuasive enough. Still, perhaps I can make one or two improvements." She then produced Her lute from out of nowhere and sang us a song with a gentle, rolling melody. At the end of Her song, She touched first my forehead, then my lips, then the middle of my chest. "It is done," She said, and faded out.

Hilary peered into my face. "Do you feel any different?"

"Not really. But then Mom didn't realize anything had happened to her 'til she nearly caused a wreck." I blinked. "You know, Hotaru, maybe this wasn't a good idea. Mom needed a lot of practice before she learned how to control her talent."

"Benzaiten would never do that to us!" my girlfriend said. "It'll be fine. *You'll* be fine." She stood on her tiptoes and kissed me, and for a moment I clung to her. This was the big time, and I'd just been given a gift of gab with no idea how to use it.

"Um," she said after a moment, "where should I sit?"

"Oh. Right." I set aside my misgivings with an effort, and recalled the circle I'd mapped out the night before.

Mom had been using a Blackfeet mediation technique called *akak'stiman* for decades; the idea is to bring not only the parties involved in the dispute into the debate, but also anyone who had a stake in the outcome, as well as those who could give historical perspective. Instead of the standard courtroom or conference-room setup you would normally see in Western mediation sessions, the Blackfeet model used a circle, for a number of reasons. For one thing, it was traditional in their tribe. But for another, it de-emphasized the idea of one person, or a handful of people, being in charge by putting all the stakeholders on an equal level.

Mom had told me all I had to do to set up the scene was to think about where everything needed to go. So I tried it. First, I imagined a big ceremonial fire in approximately the middle of the plain – and hey presto, there it was.

"Did *you* do that?" Hilary asked, her eyes wide.

"Yeah, I did," I said, blowing on my fingernails and buffing them on my shirt.

She laughed. "Okay, Mr. Big Shot. How about you conjure me a chair?"

"I can do better than that," I said, and thought of providing enough seating for a cast of millions. Benches immediately materialized all around the spot where we were standing.

"Pick a chair," I said grandly. "Any chair. Although you'll have to move again later."

She picked a bench in the front row and sat sideways, with her legs stretched along the seat. I thought up some cushiony support for her, and she threw me a grateful smile.

Now for the important parts. I brought in a table to hold the original agreement – even though Mom swore it had never been written down or formally signed, I was sure Somebody would bring a symbol we could use. The table went at the top of the circle. To its left, I provided two chairs – one each for Mom and me. Mine was the one farther from the table, as befitted the assistant to the mediator. To the right, I placed chairs for Loki and Ingun, and another for the Neo-Atheists' representative, a man named Floyd Oates who had led the guards at the Cheyenne Mountain Complex the night of our showdown in the parking lot.

Mom had told me Odin wasn't thrilled about the idea of letting Loki and Ingun loose, even for the mediation. So she had promised Him a seat on one side of the circle but right next to Loki, so the Allfather could keep an eye on His wayward foster son.

Darrell Warren would be doing the same honors for Oates, although he was to be seated on our side of the circle, together with Sage and Rafe. On the other side of them, at the bottom on our side of the circle, would sit the rest of our family: Dad, Hilary, Aunt Shannon, and Uncle George.

With Odin would be Ingrid Ingunnardottir, by virtue of her connection with Ingun, and Rex Holt. The happy couple had announced their engagement just after Thanksgiving. At the bottom of the circle on that side, I arranged a seating area with a flexible number of chairs, for whichever of the dead, the Giants, and the other deities felt they had a stake in what Loki and Ingun had wrought. And too, I expected to see at least one deity there who would want to sever the gods' connection to Earth. I didn't know who it would be, and Mom said White Buffalo Calf Pipe Woman wouldn't tell her. Maybe She wanted it to be a surprise.

In any case, I transferred the seating chart in my head to the scene before me, and was pleased to see it take shape. Just as I put the final chair in what I had privately dubbed "the surprise box," the goddess arrived with Mom, Dad, Aunt Shannon, and Uncle George. Mom stumbled a bit as she approached me, and I reached out an arm to catch her. "You okay?" I asked.

"Sure," she said. "Fine." She eased herself down in the chair I had intended for myself. "But why don't you take the lead on this one?"

I blinked. "You can't be serious."

"I'm afraid I am." Her lip curled in disgust at her frailty. "I'm sorry, honey, but I think the stress of all this has set back my recovery a little bit. I woke up this morning feeling worse than I have in days. And I know you wouldn't want me to overdo it."

"Mom," I hissed. "I can't do this alone!"

"You're not alone," she said, patting my hand. "I'll be right here next to you."

I had no way to know whether she was telling me the truth, or whether she was milking her illness as a way to get me to run the thing. Regardless, I was stuck. I shot her a glare and turned away from her.

The benches were beginning to fill up – and so were the chairs inside the circle. Sage and Rafe arrived; I shook hands with Rafe while Sage gave Mom a hug. Then she embraced me. "I bet she's faking," she murmured in my ear.

"Probably," I murmured back.

"Well, good luck," she said, louder. "If you need me to set fire to anyone, just give me a sign."

"Let's all hope it doesn't come to that," I said.

"Webb, how could you?" White Buffalo Calf Pipe Woman said behind me. "You forgot chairs for Us." I turned and beheld both my mother's goddess and Spider Grandmother.

"Sorry," I said, and thought up chairs for Them. "I didn't think You would be sitting with us." Then I turned to the Navajo goddess. "*Yá'át'ééh abiní, amá sání.* I'm glad to see You again."

"You have woven yourself quite a rug, grandson," She said.

I remembered the weaving She'd been working on when I met Her in the desert in New Mexico. "It should be nearly done by now," I said.

She laughed. "Oh, that's a good one. No, Webb, your weaving is just beginning."

I leaned in and, in a confidential tone, asked, "So, Grandmother, are you my goddess?"

"You might say we have an affinity," She said with a sly wink. "But that one has a prior claim on you." She motioned toward the bench behind my sister, where Iktomi had just slunk to a seat. He nodded to me, and then wrapped his chief's blanket around Himself and seemed to disappear. "I did bring your friend, though," She went on. She opened Her hand, and the little golden spider skittered from Her palm and onto my shoulder.

"Hey, little guy," I said with a grin. I glanced up at Spider Grandmother. "So he was from You all along?"

She nodded, smiling at the spider's antics. "I could not always get through the gate, but he was small enough to slip through and find you, no matter what."

"He's been a loyal pal," I said. "Thank You."

She nodded and took Her seat.

Jehovah floated down on his cloud and took a seat in the "surprise box." For a moment, I wondered whether he might be the deity who wanted to sever ties with Earth, after all. But no – He smiled and nodded to everyone and took a seat near the back of the box. Clearly He didn't intend to be a part of this show.

Odin arrived in his traveling cloak and porkpie hat, herding Loki and Ingun, well trussed, before Him. Ingun looked somewhat chastened, but Loki appeared ready to spit...whatever small projectiles Norse gods would spit when They were angry. Pebbles, maybe. Or twigs of mistletoe.

"Naomi," rumbled Odin, "I am only acceding to this farce because it was you who requested it of Me. I would not do this for anyone else – god or human."

"Understood, Odin, and thank You," my mother responded.

The Allfather turned to my father. "Joseph, will you guard these two miscreants?"

Dad stood. "I appreciate the offer, Odin. But I believe my son is more than equal to the task."

While this was going on, I had caught Loki's eye and mouthed the word *playpen*, and watched with satisfaction as His hands balled into fists.

"So he is," Odin said, regarding me with His single eye. "So he is." With a gesture, He loosed the bonds holding Loki and Ingun. Two ravens circled Their heads and came to light in the space between the Allfather and Loki, regarding the prisoners silently.

"Shoo," Loki muttered, but they did not. He glared at them, and then proceeded to ignore them.

Darrell brought Floyd Oates, whose handcuffs were more conventional than Loki and Ingun's had been. Darrell unlocked the cuffs and made sure the guy was seated where he belonged. Then he took a seat next to Sage and Rafe.

To my surprise, Leonard and Grandma arrived. I hurriedly provided them seats behind Hilary, Uncle George, Aunt Shannon, and Dad, and then – protocol be damned – I went over to greet them. "I didn't know you were coming," I said as I hugged my grandmother.

"Neither did we," Leonard said, "but the goddess told us we needed to be here."

A few moments later, I understood why. In trooped those who had awakened at the third cock crow – among them, the Giants, as well as Odin's beloved son Baldur and the rest of the dead. The "surprise box" wasn't that big – or so I'd thought – but it stretched to accommodate everyone. All, that is, except three: Baldur took a seat next to his father, and Grandfather and Grandpa Drew slid into our family box. This time, it was Mom who broke protocol and rushed to greet them. I couldn't hear what she said to them, but Aunt Shannon was busy handing out tissues for a few moments.

As Mom resumed her seat next to me, still dabbing at her eyes, I leaned over and whispered, "You forgot to limp."

She sniffed once, and gave me an arch smile. "Get to work," was all she said.

"Can't," I said. "Not everybody's here yet."

A moment later, Ingrid and Rex took their seats. Ingrid seemed smaller and less confident than the last time I'd seen her. "She's lost some of her pluck," I said to Mom.

"Yeah, well, having a goddess pull the rug from under you will do that," she said, side-eyeing her own goddess – whose attention, lucky for Mom, was trained on the "surprise box."

I saw why. The final participants – representing the gods who wanted to split from humanity – had arrived. Mom sucked in a breath and leaned forward. "I never would have thought of Them," she said. "Not in a million years."

"Who are They?" I'd never seen either of Them before, but They looked Mesoamerican to me. One had a long snout and wore a feathered collar; the face of the other was striped yellow and black, and one of His feet had been transformed into a black mirror.

"Quetzalcoatl," Mom said. "And Tezcatlipoca."

The Mexica brother gods argued for a moment over where to sit. At last, They elbowed Their way through the crowd of Giants and resurrected dead, and took seats front and center in the first row of the box.

"Good to see you, Naomi," Quetzalcoatl called courteously.

Tezcatlipoca nodded imperiously – first to Mom and me, and then to my sister. "I suppose I should thank you for putting Jack Rivers out of his misery," he growled.

"You're welcome for doing Your job for You," Sage retorted. "It was Your fault he was crazy in the first place."

"Yes, well, that's partly why We're here," Quetzalcoatl said, as His brother opened His mouth for an angry reply. Tezcatlipoca then crossed His arms and sat back, glowering at Quetzalcoatl. The Feathered Serpent nodded to me. "You may proceed."

"Thank You," I said, "and thank you all for coming. I'm Andrew Curtis, and I'll be conducting this mediation..."

I paused as one more person took a seat: Roman Holt. He usurped one of my hosting duties by creating his own chair. Then he leaned a guitar against the chair's back and plopped down on the seat. "Sorry I'm late," he said.

I couldn't help but smile. "You planning on busking?"

"Nah," he said. "The gods are lousy tippers. I just thought you might need some entertainment. Nobody ever thinks of hiring a band for these things. Hey, Rex! Hey, Ingrid!" He made a big show of waving merrily at them across the fire pit; neither responded.

"Are we good now?" I asked.

"Yeah, it's cool." He folded his hands across his middle and gave me a bright-eyed, expectant look.

"Let's start again," I said. "As I said a moment ago, my name is Andrew Curtis, although you may all call me Webb. With me is my mother, Naomi Witherspoon Curtis, whom you all know." I gestured toward Mom, who took a little bow from her seat. "And as you know, we are here today to address some of the issues that have come up since the original mediated settlement..." I turned to the table, which remained empty.

"Oh, right! Sorry," said Roman. He sprang out of his chair, pulled some sort of case out of his back pocket, dropped it on the table, and resumed his seat. He smoothed his bangs away from his face and took up his attentive pose again.

"What is that?" I asked.

"It's the settlement," he said. "Or an electronic copy, anyway, on a hard drive."

"It can't be. Nobody wrote it down," Mom said. She got up to inspect the drive. It turned blue as she picked it up.

"Dad had it transcribed."

"From what source? Nobody recorded..." Eyes narrowed, she looked at Loki.

I figured it out at the same time Mom did. "Just like nobody recorded what went on between you and Jack," I said.

Mom replaced the device on the table and gripped the edge, presumably to keep from slapping Him. "Even when You were on our side, You weren't on our side," she said.

"He's on no one's side but His own," said Ingun – the first time She had spoken since Her arrival. "I would like for the record to show that I am no longer affiliated with this miserable excuse for a god in any way."

"Noted," I said, unable to keep the disgust out of my voice. "Got that down, Loki?"

"It was helpful to the President," He rasped, "to have a copy of the text. I just happen to have an excellent memory and was able to recreate it for him. Can we get on with this?"

Mom threw Him one more venomous look and sat down again.

"With pleasure," I said, sneering. But then something – Benzaiten's gift, I supposed – slid between my reasoning mind and my emotions. I was instantly grateful; I desperately needed to keep a clear head. "As I was saying, we're here today to address some of the issues that have come up since the original settlement was reached thirty-eight years ago. In the intervening years, factions have come forward, both in this realm and on Earth, opposing some or all of the agreement. We're here today to clear the air, address those issues we can address, and find a way going forward that's agreeable to all."

"Why isn't Naomi speaking?" Someone in the audience called out.

"Because I'm retired," Mom said. "Webb is taking over my practice. He is a skilled negotiator, and he has balls of brass." That got a round of laughs. She grinned up at me. "And I'd say that even if he weren't my son."

"'Balls of brass!' That's going in the song," Roman said, grinning like a madman.

I was afraid to ask what song he was talking about. Instead, I raised my hand in a bid for silence, and gradually everyone calmed down. "I appreciate a good joke as much as anyone," I said, "but we're wasting time here.

"First, I'd like to ask those who don't feel the agreement is working to step forward and explain their reasoning."

"I'll go first," said Oates. He stood in front of the table and addressed the crowd as if I weren't there. "The Neo-Atheist Movement was founded on the premise that the gods don't exist." He cleared his throat and hiked up his pants. "Obviously, that's wrong. I mean, I can see all Y'all from where I'm standing, and Y'all look pretty real to me. But our main beef is that Y'all have been too hard on humanity."

"How so?" asked Odin.

"Well," he said, "Y'all won't let us do the things we did before. Life was better then. Women and minorities knew their place. And it was easier for men to make a living then – we didn't have to abide by as many rules. You can't make a profit if you have to keep following the gods' orders all the time. Rules are antithetical to humanity's success."

"You are free to do whatever you like," said White Buffalo Calf Pipe Woman. "All humans are. But there is a price to pay. Even humans who do as the gods say have to pay a price."

"That's just what I'm saying!" Oates said. "If we do what You say, we lose our freedom!"

"And what if you don't do what They say?" asked Sage. "I've seen your utopia first-hand, Floyd, and I want no part of it. You say 'women knew their place' back then – but what you really mean is they had to do whatever men told them to do."

"Your freedom was predicated on subjugating others," I said, nodding.

But Sage didn't seem to hear me. "I was raped in your utopia, Floyd Oates," she said, red lights playing in the depths of her eyes. "And regardless of whether the gods stay on Earth or leave, I pledge to make it my business that you and your kind *never* come to power again." She sat down, and Rafe took her hand.

Oates stood stiffly, as if willing himself not to give her a dressing-down. Once again, my own anger blossomed, and I felt that screen slide between the emotion and me. I closed my eyes and took three slow, centering breaths, in and out. Then I asked Oates, "What if the tables were turned? Let's say someone came into your home and forced you to do anything he told you to do. You had to sleep and eat and work on his schedule, not yours. Would you be free?"

"No," he said. "That's what I'm saying. That's what your gods have done to us!"

"None of Us has *forced* you to do anything," said Odin. "Except maybe Loki."

"Loki is who freed us!" Oates said.

"Please, Mr. Oates," I said. "Just answer my question. In the scenario I described, would you consider yourself a free man?"

"I already said no."

"How would you attain your freedom?"

"By shooting the man who took over my house," he said without a moment's hesitation.

"But then you've robbed him of *his* freedom."

"So what? I don't care about him."

"You wouldn't care about the man who enslaved you," I said.

"No."

"Would it be fair to say, then, that the only person you would care about in that scenario is yourself?"

"Of course," he said.

"And is that also true in general?" I said. "Everyone should only care about himself?" When he hesitated, I pushed my point. "What if you needed help to overthrow this man? You'd need to get a gun from somewhere, and he certainly wouldn't allow you to keep one of your own. What if he were a lot bigger and stronger than you?"

"Well…"

"If everyone only cared about themselves, how would you convince other people to help you?"

"Well…because nobody should enslave anybody else," he said.

"But it's okay if you're doing the enslaving."

"I never said that!"

"But isn't that what you mean when you say women and minorities should know their place?" I said. "The women my sister knew at the Neo-Atheists compound in Georgia were enslaved to their husbands. You think that's okay? You don't think women have the right to be free?"

"*He* told us it was okay!" he shouted, pointing at Loki.

"He used you," said Ingun. "He used Me, too. And Lucifer. And Jack Rivers."

"But why?" Oates cried.

"Because He's a psychopath," Mom said quietly.

"Because it was *fun*," Loki grated. He looked around at all the Tricksters arrayed before Him: Dad, Rafe, Roman, and me. "Don't act superior to Me. You know I'm right. And each of you has helped Me, at one time or another."

"But there's a difference," I said. "We don't set out meaning to hurt people. And if we do, we try to make it right. *You* don't care."

"He used to care," said Baldur.

"Until He set up Your brother to kill You," Odin said bitterly.

Baldur looked at His father. "The punishment You set for Him was a brutal one."

"And I released Him, because Naomi asked it of Me. And You see how He has repaid Us – by triggering Ragnarok."

"Ragnarok was going to happen again anyway," said Loki with a smirk. "I just set the clock forward a little bit."

"Three millennia is not a little bit!" Odin roared.

"May I just say," Quetzalcoatl interjected, "that this goes to the heart of why My brother and I would see Us depart from the Earth."

"Go ahead," I said.

"Thank You." Quetzalcoatl made a hissing noise; I realized He was clearing His throat. "Our view is that We have visited Our internecine wars on humanity for long enough. It's one thing for Us to tear up Our own realm; it's another thing entirely for Our troubles to spill over into the Earthly realm." He gazed at the humans assembled here. "We have caused you so much trouble."

"But you've helped Us, too," said Hilary, standing, so she could get a better look at the Feathered Serpent. "Look at what You've done on Earth in the few short years since Your return. Thirty-eight years is nothing to You, who are immortal – but it's a couple of generations to us. And in these few years, You've made Earth a wonderful place to live. No one wants for anything any more. Everyone is happy. Well, almost everyone." She eyed Oates, who glared back at her. "Some people don't know how good they have it."

"There will always be people who want more than they deserve to have," Aunt Shannon said, as Hilary sat back down. "And there will always be people who believe they deserve it all." She looked at Quetzalcoatl. "That's why we need for You to stay."

"That's why I would put in place a human," said White Buffalo Calf Pipe Woman, "to take care of such things."

"You would put in place Your own chosen human," said Ingun. "Just as You put Yourself in charge of picking Naomi as Our mediator the last time."

"Have I chosen poorly?" White Buffalo Calf Pipe Woman shot back.

"You cannot dictate to Us," said Ingun, "even as We cannot dictate to humanity. Some of Us would prefer to choose a different candidate for this so-called administrative position." She nodded at Ingrid.

"Me?" she squeaked.

"No," I said. "Your baby. Didn't She fill you in?"

The panicked look on Ingrid's face told me She hadn't, even as Ingun said, "I would nominate Ingrid Ingunnardottir to act as regent until a child of hers is of age to assume the role."

"It's an intriguing idea," said Rex in his sonorous fake baritone, "but we need time to think it over."

"No, we don't!" Ingrid hissed at him.

"But sweetheart…" he began.

She looked up, frantic. "Isn't there anyone else who could do it? I already have a nation to run."

"There was another nominee," Sage said. "But I turned Them down."

"I have in mind another," said White Buffalo Calf Pipe Woman. And a soft golden light shone from across the circle – emanating from Hilary's belly.

"No!" cried my girlfriend, struggling to stand.

"No!" I yelled, rounding on the goddess.

But it was Sage who sealed the deal. "How many times do I have to tell You? Leave our family alone!" she yelled. Thunder rumbled and crashed; lightning zigzagged across the sky, igniting something explosive in the fire pit. Flaming logs blew up out of the pit and rained down – but they did no damage, because instantly, a golden net sprang up between the attendees and the rain of fire.

Then real rain fell, cooling tempers and putting out the flames. I wondered who had sent it – until I heard Benzaiten's lute wafting over the plain. Roman grabbed his guitar and quickly picked up the tune.

And then that vast, vacant plain sprang into technicolor. Plants I'd never seen before rose from the blasted ground and, in the space of three heartbeats, bloomed in all the colors of the rainbow. Their sweet, rich scent was nearly overpowering.

But it wasn't over yet. For now, here came a trickle of water through the vegetation. It quickly cut a channel, deepened, and widened, until it nearly spanned the opening at the bottom of our circle. From there, it made directly for the fire pit.

I quickly made the pit deeper – much deeper – and wider, with rounded sides: a catchment pond, so the whole plain wouldn't flood. But there was no danger of it anyway, for Enkou was in control. He braced his flippers on one side of the pond and hoisted himself out. Then he waddled over to White Buffalo Calf Pipe Woman and said, "Kappa say no human dictator needed. We stay." He turned to the crowd and raised his flippers high. "We all stay."

I took a deep breath. "Thanks, Enkou."

"You good man," he said. "No charge." Then he hopped back into the pond.

"Well," I said. "I'm not sure we've come to any agreement…"

"I haven't had My say yet," Ingun said.

"You're right," I said. "My apologies. Go ahead."

She stood. "I have no interest in ruling Earth," She said. "I only wanted My followers back. Freya has already said She will help Me, as soon as My punishment is over. So I have no demands. I just wanted to put that *on the record*." She glowered at Loki. "And Ingrid," She said, "I hereby release you. You are under My protection no longer – unless you want to be."

"I do," said Ingrid.

Ingun's eyes opened wide. Then She smiled in wonderment, Her face aglow. "Really?"

"Yes, really." Ingrid crossed to her goddess and took Her hands. "You've always been good to me, until Loki entered the picture. So don't despair, beloved Ingun. You will always have at least one follower."

"Thank you, My dear," said the goddess, Her lower lip quivering.

I gave them a moment, and then said, "Have we resolved everything? What I'm hearing is that humans, by and large, want the gods to stay. Does that set Your minds at ease?" I asked Quetzalcoatl.

"It does," He responded, and nudged Tezcatlipoca.

"Yes, all right. Can We go now? I am sure it is Your turn to be Huitzilopochtli."

"We have been over this and *over* this," said Quetzalcoatl, exasperation in His tone. "I cannot be both Huitzilopochtli and the ruler of the Fifth Sun."

"But I am so tired of Coatlicue hugging Me!" Tezcatlipoca said. "I am always covered in snake bites!"

Quetzalcoatl looked around. "Excuse Us," He said, and the pair faded out.

Mom, Dad, and Aunt Shannon laughed. "Some things never change," Mom said.

"That's one thing resolved," I said as I turned to the goddess behind Mom. "And if the gods are staying, there's no need for a human administrator to act in Their stead. Plus we're fresh out of candidates."

"Now, we never said for sure…" Rex began.

"Yes, we did," said Ingrid, scurrying back to her seat. I half expected her to clap her hand over Rex's mouth. "Yes, we did. Thank you very much for thinking of us, but we are not interested."

"But sweetheart…" Rex said again.

"Oh, go home," said Roman, laughing, and waved a hand. Ingrid and Rex winked out.

I stared at him. "You're not just *allied* with Hermes, are you?"

"Let's just say we're very close," he said, his eyes twinkling. Then he caught up his guitar and began singing,

> And so ends my tale of the Hero of the Plain,
> The man with balls of brass!
> He showed his mettle against all the gods,
> And told them to kiss his ass!

The crowd applauded politely. It sounded like thunder.

"It needs work," I said, when the applause subsided. He bowed from his seat, put the guitar down, and smoothed the hair out of his eyes.

"So," I said, "that leaves Loki."

The god in question stared defiantly back at me.

"His punishment has already been decided," said Odin.

"Father," said Baldur. "I wish You would reconsider."

Odin sat back in surprise. "But My boy, He as good as killed You! How can You plead His case?"

"I have learned that too harsh a punishment can do more harm than good," said Baldur. "Loki will always be a Trickster. But He has served out His punishment for My death. Can You not devise some other discipline than to tie Him yet again to that rock?"

Inspiration struck. "What if You simply kept Him from getting to Earth?" I asked. "Then He would be unable to draw humans into His plots. And You can keep a pretty tight lid on Him in Your realm, can't You?"

"That is an excellent idea, Webb," said Baldur. "Do agree to try it, Father."

"Oh, all right," Odin said. "But only because it is You asking, My beautiful boy." He shook His head. "First Naomi, and now You. I must be getting sentimental in My old age."

"Never, Father," said Baldur. "You are still as strong and as tough as I remember You." Odin shook His head, but His single eye gleamed.

"Thank You, brother, for taking My side," Loki said to Baldur.

"Don't thank Me," He replied. "I spoke only from simple fairness and a recognition of Our shared godhood. If You are truly grateful, You will not waste this second chance."

"Third chance," I said. "But who's counting?"

"You are, apparently," said Loki. Then He stood and sighed. "I am ready whenever You are, Allfather."

Odin nodded. With a last look at His dead son, He rounded up both Loki and Ingun, and the three of Them headed out into the flowering plain.

I turned to Mom. "That about wraps things up, doesn't it? I don't think we need to add anything at all to the old agreement."

"Other than that Loki will stay in the gods' realm and not trouble humans any longer," said Mom. "But yes, you're right. The old agreement still holds."

I turned back to the crowd to dismiss the meeting, only to discover that the crowd had dismissed itself. The only people still with us were family: Dad, Sage and Rafe, and Hilary, of course; Aunt Shannon and Uncle George; Leonard and Grandma; and Grandfather and Grandpa Drew.

Oh, and Roman. "That was genius at the end there," he said. "Mom's gonna be so pleased when I tell her Loki's banned from Earth. But Dad's gonna be pissed."

"Glad I could help," I said. "Family harmony is my specialty. And speaking of harmony, your song sucks."

"Thanks!" he said brightly. "It'll be all over the country by this time tomorrow."

"Great," I said in dismay.

"Oh, and speaking of tomorrow," he said, "a little bird told me you'll be getting some good news."

It was the first time I'd thought about the grant in hours. "You mean my project made the first cut?" I asked.

But all he did was laugh. "See ya later, Webb," he said as he dematerialized before my eyes. "It's been real."

Grandpa Drew and Grandma were having a private moment, and everyone else was gathered around Grandfather. I squeezed in by slipping an arm around Hilary.

"The man of the hour," Dad said, clasping my shoulder. "Good work, son."

"Not exactly how I would have handled things," said Mom. "But you got the job done." She beamed at me.

"And that's why you don't want me taking over your practice," I told her. "I won't do anything the way you would do it."

She dismissed my concern with a wave of her hand. "Everyone has their own style."

"Listen to your mother," said Grandfather. "You did well. I am proud of you." As I let his words warm me inside, he turned to Sage. "And I am proud of you, too, granddaughter. I was watching you today. Your anger no longer defines you, and it gladdens my heart to see it."

She beamed. "It turns out the world's a much nicer place when you're not pissed off all the time. Who knew?" Rafe put an arm around her and gave her a kiss.

"Get a room, you two," I said with a grin, and kissed Hilary.

"And you, Hilary," Grandfather continued. "Another young woman who gladdens my heart. I see you have found your voice at last."

"She always had one," I said as I hugged her. "She just uses it more now."

"Thank you, Looks Far," she said, turning pink from the attention.

Grandpa Drew and Grandma joined us then. "So I hear wedding bells are gonna chime," Grandpa Drew said. "When's the big day?"

"Uh…" I said.

"We haven't set a date yet," said Hilary. "We've been kind of busy."

Grandfather looked crestfallen. "I no longer have the authority to perform a wedding ceremony," he said. "If I did, I would marry you right now."

"I do," Uncle George said.

"What?" That was Aunt Shannon.

"Didn't I tell you I got certified?" he said. "Must have slipped my mind."

"Look at you, George," Dad said. "You're turning into a regular shaman."

"Don't start that shit with me," said Uncle George. "Anyhow, yeah, I can do it. Just name the day."

Hilary and I traded a look. "Tomorrow?" she said with a grin. "It'll take your mind off the grant application."

"Sounds good to me," I said fervently.

Uncle George laughed. "Well, maybe not that soon. I gotta ask the boss for time off work."

"Granted," said Dad, with a coyote grin. "Let's make these two kids legal as soon as possible."

"I wish I could be there to see it," said Grandfather wistfully. "But we have to go."

Our good moods evaporated in an instant. "It has been good to see you both," I said.

"For a few stolen moments," Mom said. "We miss you." She took Grandma's hand.

"We miss you, too," Grandpa Drew said. "But we'll all be together again someday." He tried to make it sound like that was enough, but I don't think anyone was buying it. I know I wasn't.

"We have to go," said Grandfather again, and raised his hand in farewell.

"I don't know what's worse," Sage said after they had faded out. "Knowing we'll never see them again until we're dead, or seeing them for a minute." She turned her face to Rafe's shoulder.

"This wasn't long enough, that's for sure," Aunt Shannon said.

Rafe took his attention away from his wife for a moment. "Hey, Webb, how are we getting home?"

I looked around. Our beloved dead had apparently taken the last of the furniture with them; the only thing left on the technicolor plain, besides us, was Enkou's brand-new pond.

Then again, maybe it wasn't just a pond.

"I wonder…" I said, and stepped toward it.

At that moment, the kappa himself surfaced. "Yes," he said, encouraging me forward with one flipper. "This way." And he dove back under.

"I don't know about this," Uncle George said.

"No, I think it's gonna be fine," I said. "I have a feeling I know where this ends up. There's only one thing I don't know."

"What's that?" Dad asked.

"How the rest of you guys will get home," I said.

Hilary gave me a surprised grin. I took her hand and led her to the edge of the pond. "One…two…three…" we chorused, and jumped in…

…and surfaced, just as I'd suspected, in Enkou's pond in our backyard.

Chapter 13

Mom, it turned out, was an expert at pulling together a wedding on short notice. Before I could say, "Now hold on a minute," she had found us suitable clothes, called a florist, and ordered food from her favorite caterer.

"Anything else we need to do?" she said as she went over her checklist with us that night. She sat at our dinette table, where she'd been ever since we got back. She'd been forced to use actual paper and a pen for her list, as her tablet was at the house in Golden.

"Uh, Mom?" I said, trying not to grin. "Hilary's parents might like to come."

"Of course," she said, whacking herself in the forehead. "I can order their airline tickets." She looked at Hilary expectantly, and noticed her hand covering her mouth. "What?"

My bride-to-be was trying hard not to giggle. She pulled her hand down long enough to say, "I called them when you were going through my closet. They're already on their way."

"Oh," said Mom, and looked between the two of us. Then, slowly, she set down her pen. "Of course, it's your wedding, and you're perfectly capable of planning it yourselves…"

"It's not that," I said.

"…but you weren't moving very fast," she went on, "and if the ceremony's tomorrow…"

"Mom," I said, placing my hands on hers. I crouched next to her and said, "It's okay. We've got this. You just get the house ready."

"Food," she said.

"Yes."

"And flowers."

"That would be terrific," said Hilary. "Thank you, Mom."

"Okay. You're welcome. We should go." She folded her checklist and slipped it into a pocket. Then she got up, took three steps, and dropped.

Thank the gods I was there to catch her. "Mom? Are you okay?" I asked as Hilary ran to the backyard to get Dad.

"Fine," she said, with a sound halfway between a laugh and a gulp. "Just tired, that's all."

Aunt Shannon outpaced my father. I'd barely gotten Mom onto the couch with her feet up when our personal practitioner laid hands on her. She heaved a sigh of relief and straightened. "It's exhaustion," she pronounced.

"I said I was tired," Mom said. "Don't fuss over me."

"When did you eat last?" Aunt Shannon turned to the group now gathered in our living room: her husband, Sage and Rafe, Dad, and Hilary and me. "My gods – when did *any* of us eat last?"

"I can fix that," Sage said, pulling out her phone. "We'll order something."

"Nothing rich for your mother," Shannon said.

"For gods' sake, Shannon!" Mom yelled. "I'm fine!"

After dinner, Hilary got everybody into her car somehow and drove them to Golden – all except Sage and Rafe, who decided to spend one more night at their old college crash pad before we turned the guest room into a nursery. Rafe went off to check his email, leaving Sage and me in the living room, waiting for Hilary to come home.

"Question for you," I said, as I nursed a cup of coffee.

"Shoot."

"This has been bugging me all afternoon," I confessed. "Do you think our kid will be normal?"

She gave me a sly grin. "You mean because you're the father? You should have thought of that much sooner, little brother."

"Y'know, it's nice that some things never change," I said. "You've never been funny, and you still aren't." She stuck her tongue out at me, which was the reaction I was going for. "What I meant was this: when we were all busy telling the goddess that we didn't want to raise Earth's next dictator for Her, She did something to Hilary that made her belly glow."

"Yeah, I remember that."

"So do you think...?"

Sage shrugged. "I have as little experience with this as you do, Webb. The impression I've always had was that Mom and Dad changed or morphed or something when you and I were each conceived, and that's why we turned out the way we have. You haven't been possessed by Anybody while you were having sex with Hilary, have you?"

"That's an awfully personal question," I said in mock outrage.

She raised an eyebrow. "So the answer is no."

"Right."

"Yeah. Me neither. Although we've been trying very hard *not* to have a baby all these years, so maybe it's not quite the same thing."

We were skating close to TMI territory, but I said, "It wasn't like *we* were trying to get pregnant, either."

"I figured." She sat back. "Anyway, I don't know what to tell you. One coat of glow-in-the-dark shellac shouldn't be enough to grant the kid super powers, but then taking into account that you're already stoked..." She trailed off. "And Rafe and I both..." She shook her head. "I guess we'll all have to wait and see."

"Great. Thanks for doing so much to put my mind at ease."

She grinned. "It's what I'm here for."

The wedding ceremony was lovely, of course – or at least, that's what I've been told. It was warm enough for about fifteen minutes at midday for Uncle George to do the honors on my parents' deck. That quarter-hour passed in a blur – something about loving and taking care of Hilary forever, which I had already planned to do anyway. We got a few photos before everyone began to turn blue. Then we hurried back inside for food.

I'd met Hilary's parents once before. Toshiro Takahashi had retired from Qualcomm when it was still Qualcomm, and his wife

Naoki had been in health care tech. So they were both very science-oriented; they had more in common with Sage and Rafe than with me. They were also somewhat awed, I think, by the family their only daughter had just married into. We talked about how much her mother's first name was like my mom's — only one letter different! — and the conversation kind of ran out of steam after that.

I was beginning to hope my kid developed an interest in the arts, just so I'd have somebody in the family to talk to.

I was just about to suggest to Hilary that we take our leave and let the party go on without us when my phone rang with the warble I have reserved for numbers I don't recognize. Normally I let those calls go to voicemail, but something prompted me to pick this one up.

"Andrew Curtis?" the pleasant voice on the other end of the line asked.

"This is he. Could you hang on a minute? It's really noisy in here." I scooted out the front door and stood on the porch. The temperature had nosedived over the past couple of hours, and the air tasted like snow. "Okay, thanks for holding. Yes, this is Andrew Curtis. How can I help you?"

"Mr. Curtis, I'm Donna Friedrich with the Colorado Committee for the Preservation of the Arts," the woman chirped.

My heart sank. I had really, really been hoping I wouldn't hear from them today. "Hi," I managed. Then I frowned. "I'm sorry. What did you say your name was?"

"Donna Friedrich."

"That's what I thought you said." Despite the cold, I hiked my butt up onto the railing that ran the length of the porch. "Well, I'm honored to hear from you, Ms. Friedrich. Usually when I don't make the cut, I get a call from a low-level flunky, not the committee chair — if I'm lucky." I paused, as she had begun to laugh. "Okay," I said, smiling a little. "Want to let me in on the joke?"

"I'm not calling to reject your project," she said. "I'm calling to congratulate you."

"I…I won?" I slid slowly off the railing and came to my feet. "But how is that possible? I mean, the winner isn't supposed to be announced for another couple of weeks."

"The committee liked your project so much that we've decided to honor it with a special award – the Kurt and Elinor Lange Award. We don't give out the Lange Award every year – only when we receive a project that we believe merits it."

"So it's nothing I could have applied for separately."

"That's correct."

"Well, this is quite an honor," I said. "Although I confess I've never heard of this particular prize."

"I'm not surprised. It's been many years since we received an application for a project of the caliber of yours."

"Thank you," I said automatically – and then it clicked. "Wait. Kurt Lange. As in Mjollnir Exploration? *That* Kurt Lange?"

It was her turn to be surprised. "You've heard of him?"

"You could say there's a family connection." I shook my head. "So Ms. Friedrich, not to be crass, but what do I win?"

She laughed again. "Of course. The award comes with a stipend, courtesy of an endowment from the Lange estate." When she named the amount of the stipend, I had to sit down again; it was equal to a couple of years' worth of Hilary's salary.

"No kidding," I said faintly.

"No kidding," she said. "Congratulations again, Mr. Curtis. I'll let you get back to your party."

"Reception," I said. "I got married today."

"Well, double congratulations, then," she said. "This has been quite the day for you."

"No kidding," I repeated, and ended the call. I stared at my phone for a minute. Then I checked my received calls. No, I hadn't been hallucinating – the committee chair had indeed called and given me a thank-you gift from the gods.

"Webb?" Hilary stepped out onto the porch. "What are you doing out here? Wow, it got cold fast." She rubbed her upper arms briskly.

I drew her into my arms. "Never mind that," I said. "I just got a call from the chair of the grant committee."

"Oh, no," she said in dismay. "Wait. The *chair* called?"

"Yup," I said. "I won!" And I filled her in on what I knew so far. "You know what this means, right?"

"It means you won't have to work for your mother for at least another couple of years," she said.

"That, too. But you know what else it means?"

"No. What?"

"It means you're writing all of my grant applications from now on."

"If that's what it takes," she said, "I'll do it gladly. Now let's go back inside. It's freezing out here."

"Good idea," I said, dropping my voice an octave and pulled her close. "Because I've got something I need to show you, baby."

"I've already seen it," she said with a laugh, pressing a hand to her belly. Then she gave me a fetching smile. "But I wouldn't mind seeing it again. In fact, I'd like to see it every day for the rest of my life."

"Deal," I said, and kissed her.

What came after

Sora Virginia Curtis made her debut just a few days before Christmas, on December twenty-first – the winter solstice. We were all aware of the significance of the day; my mother had received her marching orders from the goddess on the winter solstice of 2012.

But Sora seemed blessedly normal for a four-day-old baby. Which is to say she mostly ate and pooped and cried and slept. If she had any unusual ability, it wasn't apparent yet.

Of course, it's possible that her mother and I were so tired that we missed it.

Months later, when I was building my project, I would sometimes take the baby with me to the site so Hilary could get some work done. The site we settled on, by the way, was the Ute tribal property where Grandfather's wickiup had once stood. The human operators of the carbon dioxide reclamation facility had improved his old driveway to a less-suicidal grade, and neither they nor the gods seemed to mind having my project nearby. If Grandfather minded, I never heard about it.

Anyway, I usually wore the baby in a sling when I took her up there, but sometimes I'd let her roam a little – never letting her get too close to the edge of the cliff, of course. On some of these occasions, Sora would raise her tiny face to the sun and smile as if she saw Someone there who pleased her. But no one ever materialized, so it was hard to tell.

Maybe she just liked the sunshine on her face.

In any case, that came later. On that first Christmas, she was tiny and new, and everyone was charmed by her.

"She's gorgeous," Sage murmured as our little bundle of joy nodded off on her shoulder.

"You look real natural with that baby," I said to my sister.

"Shut the fuck up, Webb," she said.

But later, after Hilary took Sora off Aunt Sage's hands and retired to feed her, my sister cornered me in the living room.

"Promise you won't tell a soul," she said. "*Especially* not Mom and Dad."

"Not 'til you tell me what it is," I said. "You know how this works."

"No, come on."

"Oh, all right, fine," I said. "What is it?"

She leaned over and whispered in my ear, "I'm pregnant."

I couldn't help it. I was unnaturally gleeful when I whispered back, "I know."

A little while later, I shrugged on my coat and stepped onto the back deck to get some air.

Memories flooded my senses: the scent of wood smoke as Grandfather sat by the fire pit, telling Sage and me stories when we were little; the mouth-watering aroma of charcoal and meat juices as Dad presided over the grill while Mom set out plates and cups on the table; the smell of pine sap and fresh air as Sage chased me across the bridge and all the way to Grandfather's yurt, now long gone; a brisk hint of snow at my own wedding, a few weeks before. So much of my life was wrapped up in this place. And now my daughter's life would be wrapped up in it, too.

As I turned to go back inside, I noticed a giant spider web strung from the edge of the woodpile to the deck railing. There was no message in it this time – nor did there need to be. All it needed to be was perfect. And it was.

Author's Note

No, really – this is it: the final *Pipe Woman Chronicles* book. I wrote the first draft of *Seized* for my NaNoWriMo project in November 2011, and this series has occupied my writing life (other than *Seasons of the Fool* and some short stories for the Five59 anthologies) ever since.

To give you an idea of how long ago that was, I was writing then for the Indie Exchange, which no longer exists, and Indies Unlimited was barely more than a twinkle in the Evil Mastermind's eye. (Whoa. I just realized I've been writing for IU for four years. And I'm *still* getting sloppy seconds at the gruel pot. Note to self...)

My original intent with this series was not just to explore what would happen if the gods came back, but also to imagine a world in which things like fear, greed, and suffering no longer existed. One thing I've learned along the way is that you can stamp out the bad stuff for a while, but because humans are, well, human, maintaining that kind of world requires constant vigilance. For those of us who live in a less-than-perfect world, that's not a bad reminder.

Clay Notah's retelling of the Navajo creation story is condensed from the story I found at:

http://navajopeople.org/blog/navajo-creation-story-the-first-world-nihodilhil-black-world/

The link leads to the story about the First World; scroll down the page to find links for the stories about the other three worlds.

If I thanked everybody who deserves my thanks over the course of this series, we'd be here for another hundred pages or so. So I'll limit this note to the folks who have helped me with this book: Susan Strayer and Kat Milyko, who have once again taken on the Herculean editorial task of keeping me from looking like an idiot, and have discharged it with their usual aplomb; Amy Milyko, for the book cover consultation, and for her indulgence when I closeted myself in my writer's garret for two straight weekends to finish the first draft; the minions at Indies Unlimited – particularly K.S. Brooks, Laurie

Boris, Melissa Bowersock, Big Al, and Shawn Inmon – for their friendship, help, and advice (I was just kidding about the sloppy seconds, Kat!); Shawn again, for starting the 120 Club on Facebook, thereby forcing me to think about writing every day (even when I don't actually do it); Leland Dirks and Nicole Storey, for introducing my work to their own fans; my friends at Kevinswatch.com, for general moral support, thought-provoking discussions, and entertainment when I probably should have been writing; Michael Flynn, for the conversation we had in Ireland that I never managed to work into the book (maybe next time); and the folks on my Woo-Woo Team, for just being generally awesome.

Which reminds me: you, too, can join my Woo-Woo Team. We meet on Facebook at:

https://www.facebook.com/groups/WooWooTeam/

You have to ask to join, but so far I've let everybody in, so your odds of acceptance are spectacular. I'd love to see you there.

To get the first word on all of my new releases, please go to http://eepurl.com/xxw9d to sign up for my spam-free newsletter. I'll also post the info at my blog and on my Facebook page, but the newsletter is your guaranteed way to find out what's coming up.

One more thing: If you enjoyed *Turtle's Weir* – or even if you didn't – won't you please go back where you purchased the book to post a review? Reviews are a key way that readers find good books, and I treasure each and every review that my books receive. Thank you in advance!

Lynne Cantwell
June 2016

About the Author

Lynne Cantwell writes mostly urban fantasy and paranormal romance, with a dash of magic realism when she's feeling more serious. She is also a contributing author for Indies Unlimited. In a previous life, she was a broadcast journalist who worked at Mutual/NBC Radio News, CNN, and a bunch of other places you have probably never heard of. She has a master's degree in fiction writing from Johns Hopkins University. Currently, she lives near Washington, D.C.

Stand-Alone Novels

SwanSong
The Maidens' War
Seasons of the Fool

Contributor

Indies Unlimited 2012 Flash Fiction Anthology
Indies Unlimited 2013 Flash Fiction Anthology
Indies Unlimited 2014 Flash Fiction Anthology
Indies Unlimited Tutorials and Tools for Prospering in a Digital World
Indies Unlimited Tutorials and Tools for Prospering in a Digital World, Vol. II
BookGoodies How to Write A Book
First Chapters
13 Bites
Summer Dreams
Boo!: Volume 2
Winter Tales
Plan 559 from Outer Space
Other Realms
13 Bites Vol. III
I Heard It on the Radio
Plan 559 from Outer Space Mk. II

Find Lynne on Teh Intarwebz:

Facebook: http://www.facebook.com/pages/Lynne-Cantwell
Twitter: http://twitter.com/lynnecantwell
Google Plus: http://plus.google.com/+LynneCantwell
Goodreads:
http://www.goodreads.com/author/show/696603.Lynne_Cantwell
Blog: http://www.hearth-myth.com